# Boarlander Silverback

Boarlander Silverback
ISBN-13: 978-1530969982
ISBN-10: 1530969980
Copyright © 2016, T. S. Joyce
First electronic publication: February 2016

T. S. Joyce
www.tsjoycewrites.wordpress.com

### NOTE FROM THE AUTHOR

This book is a work of fiction. The names, characters, places, and incidents are products of the writer's imagination or have been used fictitiously and are not to be construed as real. Any resemblance to persons, living or dead, actual events, locale or organizations is entirely coincidental. The author does not have any control over and does not assume any responsibility for third-party websites or their content.

Published in the United States of America

First digital publication: February 2016
First print publication: April 2016

# Boarlander Silverback

## (Boarlander Bears, Book 3)

## T. S. Joyce

# ONE

Alison Holman was definitely going to get maimed today.

She blew out a trembling breath and gripped her Glock 22 harder to steady her shaking hands. Above, more than a dozen buzzards circled in a tight group low to the ground. They would land soon, but before they found whatever had them on the hunt, she needed to make sure the shifters here weren't into something that would bring war to Damon's mountains.

It was hot and muggy, and even with her dull human senses, she caught a whiff of rot on the wind. Her hands were shaking again, and now fear was slowly freezing her blood. This was why she'd been given this shithole job. She wasn't good under pressure. Not anymore.

When birds flew up from the knee-high

grass in front of her, she startled hard and gasped. Good thing she didn't have her finger on the trigger because she would've fired. Stupid Finn for being in town on a supply run. And stupid town for being so far away. And stupid life for leading her here to this terrifying moment.

She felt watched.

She always felt watched.

*Breathe.*

Angling her body, Alison stepped carefully out of the meadow and into the shadows of the pines. There. An animal, a deer maybe, had been killed, and the long slash marks down the back end said it was likely a bear. No, not just a bear, but a grizzly shifter. The monsters in these mountains would've pushed any predators out of the area.

It was too quiet. There were no chirping birds or soft *rush, rush* of the grass. The breeze dipped to an eerie stillness, and the fine hairs lifted all over her body. She resisted the urge to check the load in her weapon. She'd needed to make sure the monsters hadn't killed a human, but now it dawned on her what she'd stepped into—a grizzly kill. And that half-eaten prey was something an apex predator would be fiercely protective of.

She should leave. Now.

Gritting her teeth, she backed away slowly, but froze when she saw movement through the trees. Just a flash of coal-black fur, and then a massive gorilla came charging through the trees. Alison couldn't move, couldn't breathe, couldn't do anything other than watch the terrifying speed and power with which the silverback ran toward her.

*Run, run, run!*

With a horrified gasp, she stumbled back a step and tripped on a tree root. She hit the ground hard, and with a grunt, she pulled the trigger. *Boom!*

The gorilla didn't even slow down. She'd missed, and now she would die. He peeled back his dark lips, exposing long canines a second before he skidded to a stop. He slammed his fists to the ground on either side of her head so hard the earth shook. His barrel chest heaved as he inhaled deeply. He opened those terrifying jaws, then roared a deafening sound.

Covering her ears, Alison closed her eyes and waited. Waited for him to end her, waited to breathe her last breath. Maybe it was better this way. She wouldn't be in purgatory anymore.

*Just do it.*

Something warm splatted against her shoulder. *Pit, pat, pit, pat.* Why wasn't he killing her? She wanted to scream at him, "Hurry up!" Fear was the worst part of living.

With a whimper, she cracked open her eyes, and he was there, above her, more massive than she remembered from the night in the woods when she'd first met the Boarlanders. Kirk Slater was terrifying, enormous...beautiful. His eyes weren't the soft brown she would've expected in a silverback, but were instead an intense, glowing gold. She lay trapped in his gaze as the warmth she'd felt earlier was now trickling in a steady stream from his shoulder. She hadn't missed after all. Her stomach curdled with what she'd done.

"I-I'm sorry." Her voice was too frail and weak. God, she was so sick of being weak. Stronger, she said, "I'm *so* sorry."

Kirk blew out a breath, then, after a moment of hesitation, brushed her short hair from her face with a surprisingly gentle touch. His eyes softened as he ran his dark knuckle down her neck and collar bone to her bare arm. She'd been jogging when she'd seen the vultures, so she wasn't in her uniform. She was in a tank top, and now his focus was on the half-sleeve of tattoos on her arm. She moved quickly to cover as much as she could with her empty hand. Those were for her and no one else.

With a loaded look she didn't understand, Kirk punched off his powerful arms and backed away from her. He sat near a towering pine and canted his head slowly, watching her as if he'd never seen a woman cower before. Tricky monster. She knew better than to believe him soft.

He ran his fingers over the seeping wound on his shoulder, eyes on her with his chin tucked to his chest, then with an expressive frown, he looked at his crimson-smeared fingertips. He was giving her a chance to escape, so she scrambled up and holstered her weapon, then put her hands out as she backed away slowly.

He allowed it.

Alison didn't understand. She'd shot him. Hurt him, but he was allowing her safe passage? It had to be a trick. Maybe this was the game—let her think she'd escaped, then charge her and pluck her head from her body like a grape from a stem. He was strong enough to do that.

But the questions...

Why had he charged her in the first place? That deer wasn't his kill unless he grew bear claws, so what, or who, was he protecting? And then there was the little problem of her guilt over shooting him, making her legs feel like cement blocks she had to drag through the meadow. She stopped, and the silverback narrowed his eyes.

"I saw the vultures. I had to make sure no one was hurt. That's part of the job description."

He huffed what sounded like an empty animalistic laugh.

"I didn't pick this job, just so you know. I'm not here because I want to hurt you."

Kirk held two bloody fingers out and gave her a dead look. Right.

"I thought you were going to...you know...kill me. You have teeth and strength." She gestured to her holster. "This is my only weapon." She shifted her weight from side to side, debating. "I have first aid at my cabin. I can help."

Kirk blinked slowly and turned his face away, but he was holding his shoulder now, and she knew the pain he was hiding. She'd seen it before. The tuna fish sandwich she'd had for lunch threatened to come back up. She'd done that—hurt him.

"C-can I see if there is an exit wound?"

Kirk shot her a quick glance, then sat stoically, staring off into the woods as though the surrounding pine trees were the most interesting thing he'd ever seen. She knew what he was doing. He had positioned himself between her and the deer carcass, blocking her view of it completely.

Alison dragged in a deep breath and held it, then approached slowly. God, this was a bad idea. A stupid, terrible, awful idea, and yet here she was, taking step after step toward a Changed, injured shifter. And not just some bird shifter, either. No, she'd chosen one of the biggest, baddest shifters of them all. "Please don't kill me," she murmured.

Kirk turned his back on her, and she would've thought this was his tactic to ignore her so she would be on her way, but from here, she could see his shoulder, and unfortunately, it was intact, which meant she hadn't shot clean-through. He still had metal in him. Shit on a stick. This was bad, bad, bad.

"Kirk, you still have the bullet in you and—"

The titan silverback grunted and shrank

into his human form, his back still to her. She'd only seen pictures of his face, but she stumbled to a stop at the view of his wide shoulders. His arms were defined and his waist tapered, and as he stood, his powerful legs and ass were on display. Holy hell, he was beautiful, if that word could be given to a man as masculine and dominant as him. With a grunt, Kirk's back muscles jumped. He held out his hand at an angle away from himself, opened his palm, and a small, misshapen ball of metal fell from his red fingertips.

Kirk's hair was longer, shoulder-length, and mussed in that just-woke-up look she'd always found eternally sexy. He turned his face, giving her his profile, and in a hoarse voice, he ground out, "You don't have to worry about the Boarlanders. Your trigger-happy secret is safe with me."

"I..." Fuck, what could she even say? Another apology didn't do justice to what she felt inside.

"Leave," Kirk demanded. In a softer voice, he murmured, "Please."

But just the thought of leaving him like this made her sneakers feel like tree roots. Unable to move, Alison pushed for more time with him. "The kill. It's not yours."

Kirk rounded and strode toward her, his massive dick swinging with every powerful step. Holy shit, he'd looked good from behind, but his front was even better. He had long, muscular legs, eight-pack abs that flexed with every heaving breath, and a ripped chest. It wasn't until her attention shifted to the stream of blood down his left pec that she began to feel guilty at checking him out. And when she lifted her gaze to his gloriously pissed-off face, she knew she'd made a misstep in staying. She should've left when she had the chance.

"You want to know who is to blame for that animal's death back there?" Kirk asked in a dangerous, gravelly voice as he stopped right in front of her, so close she could feel his warmth.

Alison still hadn't figured out how to convince her legs to move, so she angled her head all the way back to look up at him and whispered, "Who?"

"You," he gritted out. "I assume you've done all your research on us, right? The shifters in these mountains are just pieces of paper with stats. Does your research tell you what Harrison has been through?"

"Well..."

"Tell me, and I swear to God if I hear a lie

in your voice, I'll tell the dragon you put a bullet in me."

She gulped at the seriousness of his threat. In no way, shape, or fashion did she want Damon Daye to learn of this. He would burn her and eat her ashes, just like he did to anyone who got in his way.

"Harrison Lang grew up in an abusive household," she said softly. "Mom died when he was young, and dad got more violent after she did."

"Right. And then he grew up and got a crew under him because his animal needed it. And do you know what he did? He didn't lash out like his father had taught him was right. He took a bunch of fucked-up bears and made them as safe as possible because you and your people can't seem to stop shooting at us. When you and your asshole partner came in the night for Emerson, weapons pulled like fucking cowboys, you had your guns pointed at two people who barely survived multiple bullet wounds."

"Two people," she whispered, horrified.

"Georgia of the Gray Backs and Harrison, alpha of the Boarlanders, were poached."

"Poached?" The word tasted bitter on her tongue.

"Humans paid a guide to bring them up here and *hunt* the Boarlanders. Along with Georgia, Harrison cut them off, protected the crew, but sacrificed themselves in the process. She was human, he was a bear, and now they both have matching scars, inside and out."

"And then we came in the night, threatening them," Alison murmured. Bile crept up the back of her throat, and she swallowed over and over, trying not to retch in front of him.

Kirk jammed his finger at the half-eaten deer. "That is the result of a spiraling grizzly who was fine before you came along. You want to survive this job you've been recruited to do? Try getting to know us." Kirk spat in the grass and strode off. Over his shoulder he barked out, "Next time, leave your damned weapon at home."

# TWO

Kirk was stretching his aching arm over his head when Harrison whistled so loud it echoed through the mountains. Lunch break was over. Thirty minutes had come and gone like a blink of an eye, and Kirk tossed the half-eaten sandwich in his hand a dirty look. He'd completely zoned out. What the hell was wrong with him?

He snorted. Alison Holman was what was wrong with him, probably because she shot him. He shook his head at his bullshit justification for why she was on his mind. Try to blame it on his sore, shot-up shoulder all he wanted to, but the fact was, he was intrigued by the woman. She was thin as a whip, which he usually wasn't attracted to, and all tatted up. Another negative before she'd come guns a-blazin' into his life, and now he couldn't stop

16

thinking about the intricate designs on her arm. She'd been wearing a white tank top, and her ink had gone all the way from her elbow to her collar bone and disappeared down the back of her shirt. He bet she was all painted up. He'd pegged her for a tough girl the first night she'd come for Emerson. A sexy, hard-souled, tough girl. But no. That wasn't right because she'd given Emerson information that had provided her with a loophole to marry Bash. But why?

He chucked his sandwich into the brown paper bag with the rest of his uneaten lunch and stood. Dusting his pants, he remembered how soft her skin had been under his knuckle. She'd flinched away from him looking at her tattoos, but there had been that moment where she'd been silk under his touch. She wasn't hard at all. Weapon wielding, tatted-up badass with her chopped, bleach platinum blond hair, delicate, animated, dark eyebrows, and her hard little pixie face. She'd smelled sad. And regretful after she'd pulled the trigger.

Good.

At his callousness, a long, low rumble echoed up his throat from his animal. He would never hurt a woman, but damn, he'd been pissed she'd been nosing around Harrison's kill. Nosy cop. Her partner was an easy read. Here because he wanted to put shifters in their place. Full of bravado and thinking his badge kept him safe. Alison was different, though. She was a mystery his gorilla was suddenly and overwhelmingly eager to solve.

Kirk picked up his chainsaw from where he'd set it on the ground and followed the Boarlanders down the hillside toward the trees they still had to cut. They'd been talking all through lunch, but he hadn't paid attention to a damned word. Mostly because Clinton was ranting again, and Kirk usually checked out when he went off. His issue this week? He was convinced the government was going to snuff them out of existence. They might, but hell, Clinton didn't have to breathe constant life into the thought.

Nonchalantly, Kirk asked, "What do you guys think about the cops?"

"Brackeen and Holman?" Mason asked, hopping over a thin log. "Trouble."

"I second trouble," Bash said quick, lifting his hand like he was voting for second grade class president.

Kirk grinned and ruffed up his hair. "What

else do you think, Bash bear?"

"I like Holman's hair, and she has good posture. Brackeen is a dickweed. He reminds me of Clinton."

Clinton was in front of them, but he graced them with an over-the-shoulder middle finger.

"I think we need to be wary with them," Harrison said low, sounding troubled. "The woman smelled terrified of us, but she was still steady with that Glock. A dangerous combo."

"Why do you think they're really here?" Mason asked.

Harrison shook his head and climbed over a pile of felled lumber. "Nothing good. To watch us and give intel, maybe."

"Definitely they'll make our lives hellish," Clinton muttered. "People have to check in with them like we live in some damned gated community? It ain't like people are flooding up here. If they come, it's because they're invited We should kill them."

"No!" Kirk barked out, too loud and way too fast.

Clinton turned around and stared at him as if he'd lost his damned mind, which he had. "Okay, boy scout. Get Damon to eat them then."

Mason groaned. "Clinton, you're so dumb it gives me a headache. You heard Cora. She said *keep* Damon from eating people, not feed people to him."

"Who would know?"

"Whoever sent them here, dumbass!" Harrison griped, swatting at a fly with his yellow hardhat before he put it back on his head. "No more suggestions from you."

"We could be friends with them," Bash said.

"People like them can't be friends with people like us," Harrison said softly. "They're here for bad reasons, Bash. A friendship with them wouldn't benefit us. It would give them intel. It would give them power over us. We would care about them right up until the moment they pulled the trigger on us."

Kirk swallowed hard and wiped his chin on his throbbing shoulder. Harrison was right. Alison hadn't even hesitated. She'd come weapon drawn and been fine using it on him.

"But if we were friends, maybe they wouldn't want to pull that trigger," Bash murmured. "I like friends. Not enemies. Me and Emerson got a cub comin'. Don't want no danger."

Kirk smiled and gripped Bash's shoulder.

"Don't worry, man. She and your cub are safe. She's got all our protection."

"Not mine," Clinton said lightly. He ripped the cord of his chainsaw and went to work cutting a wedge from a tree.

Kirk shook his head. Bullshit. Clinton would throw himself in front of a moving train if it would save Audrey and Emerson from hurt. He just didn't want to admit he cared about them or anyone else.

Kirk made it a safe distance away and pulled the cord of his own chainsaw. His arm hurt with the motion, and for the hundredth time, he remembered the look on Alison's face when she'd realized she shot him. Sad, disappointed, and so damned beautiful.

He didn't give a shit about her partner, Finn Brackeen, but Alison had drawn his animal straight up when she'd held her ground at his charge. She was brave, and under that tough-woman exterior, she harbored a surprising submissiveness that made no sense to him.

All of his first impressions of her had been wrong, and now he wanted to know more. Wanted to know everything. That was terrifying.

Being part of Kong's family group had

stifled his urge to choose a mate. Being under a more dominant silverback did that. But being around the Boarlanders was changing everything. Logging season was almost over, and he would go back to the Lowlanders. He balked against the idea, but it would be best. The woman he was unsettlingly interested in could be the most dangerous decision he could make for the Boarlanders.

And they deserved better.

# THREE

"Damon Daye has put off a meeting with us for two weeks now," Alison said into the phone.

Porter had been the one who'd gotten her off desk work and into this job. Sure, it was a crappy gig, but it was better than pushing papers all day. At least she was out on the streets again...er...the forest.

"Well, push the issue because you have to build up some kind of rapport with these *people*." The way he had said "people" grated on her nerves, like they were animals instead. Understandable since she'd come here thinking the same thing, but after two encounters with some of the shifters of Damon's mountains, now she wasn't so sure.

"Porter, I don't really know what I'm supposed to be doing here," she admitted.

"Brackeen and I have been told so little, and he seems fine with that, but I want clearer boundaries on this job."

"So, you're bored."

She laughed and leaned on the kitchen counter of her cabin, crossed one arm under her elbow as she held the cell phone closer. "Well, it's a different pace here than in Chicago, that's for sure."

"Enjoy the sunshine and fresh air, Holman."

"Is this to help with the problems I had before? Is this like a rest and relaxation job? Because I have to tell you, the rest of the world seems to have its prejudices with the shifters, but Saratoga seems pretty docile. Pro-shifter, in fact. The shifters don't have a single late permit, certificate, damned speeding ticket. They're clean, Porter, and from what I can tell, they are just up here trying to live their lives. So that's it, right? Send me on this bullshit job to give me some time to get over what happened?" She would rather log roll in poison ivy than talk about what had taken her from active duty, but she had so many questions about what the higher-ups wanted her doing out here, and Porter had been a slippery little bugger with his answers lately.

"Up there trying to live their lives—except for Damon killing an entire secret branch of the damned government. The Breck Crew outed that shit, Holman. Outed a top secret group to the public, and it looks bad for everyone who even smells of IESA. But that doesn't negate the fact that Damon played hungry dragon with actual living people."

"Yeah, I know. I get it. Justice and all." But was it justice if they were just defending themselves? Because she'd defended herself, and everyone on the force had said that was okay and she shouldn't feel guilt. But there seemed to be a double standard with shifters because of the animal's that resided within them.

"Eye on the prize, Holman. Don't go all sympathizer on me. You're there to keep peace, for them and for humans."

"Okay, I know. I'm the point of contact between the outside world and them."

"Exactly. You'll do great, and eventually you'll come back, and we'll get you back on the streets."

Back on the streets—that statement held a terrifying combination of words. Back undercover, he meant. Back in the darkness. Back where no one could save her fast enough when things went bad. Back to being alone with real monsters. She closed her eyes against the memories that scratched at her mind, begging for a replay. Not here, not now. Not ever if she could help it.

The throaty rumble of a car sounded outside. Probably a groupie wanting to get up into the mountains for a picture with a shifter. The shifters had a massive fan base here. "I have to go. I have to check someone in." And sadly, it would be the most exciting thing that happened all day.

"Head down, focus on that endgame," Porter said. "Babysit those shifters and then get back to normal life."

She hung up and huffed a humorless laugh. Normal life meant the mean streets of Chicago, a shitty, rat-infested apartment too close to the trains, her life at risk every day, and the constant internal reminder to not let herself get too close to anyone. People who got too close to her had short expiration dates.

On that dark thought, she pushed off the counter and sauntered through the small living area to the front door. Her cabin had the office sign on it, so she got to turn away the groupies. Lucky her. She didn't even know what the hell Brackeen did all day.

She hooked her badge to the waist of her jeans, pulled open the door, and put on her neutral business face, which fell straight off when she saw who had pulled into the circle drive in front of her cabin.

A shiny green Mustang with black racing stripes, and leaned up against it like he'd been there all day was none other than Kirk Slater. Hole-riddled jeans graced his long legs, one foot crossed over the other, and a V-neck white T-shirt clung to his torso like a second skin. Dark two-day stubble dusted his chiseled jaw, and his dark eyes narrowed at her. Huh, his eyes weren't the glowing gold of his silverback, but a soft brown instead. "Damon is ready to see you."

"Oh," she said, surprised. "Uhuh, I have to wait for my partner to come back."

"He isn't interested in meeting your asshole partner. Just you."

"So, let me get this straight. You want me to drive deep into the heart of the dragon's mountains without my partner. Without backup."

Kirk laughed and shook his head. "We ain't at war with you, Alison."

"Ally." She cleared her throat as her cheeks heated. Why the hell had she said that? "My

27

friends call me Ally."

"Lie."

Oh yeah, she forgot about that whole built-in lie-detection instinct shifters had. "I wished my friends called me Ally."

Kirk canted his head and frowned. "Half-truth."

Alison closed her eyes as her mortification burned over her cheeks and up to her ears. "I don't have many friends, but if I did, I would like them to call me Ally."

Kirk waited a few moments too long in his response to be polite, and when he did talk, all he said was, "Get in." Then he pulled his door open and slid in behind the wheel.

Get in? She cast a glance back at her cabin. Her holster was hung by the door.

Kirk rolled down the window. "Ally, if you want a ride to the dragon's lair, get in now. No weapons, or you'll piss me and everyone else off there. I won't let anything happen to you."

"And I'm supposed to just trust you?"

"Have I given you any reason not to?" he asked, dark brows jacked up.

"I don't trust anyone. Force of habit."

"That's a sad story. Now get your ass in my car before I drag you in here. I don't want you traipsing all over the mountainside alone looking for Damon. The Gray Backs won't be as nice as my crew." His brows lowered. "I mean the Boarlanders, not my crew."

This was a terrible idea, but Brackeen was down in Saratoga, again, and she'd been vying for this meeting with Damon since the day she'd arrived. And though she wouldn't admit it out loud, a deep buried instinct told her Kirk was safe. Which was ridiculous because he'd probably told his crew about her shooting him, and he was most likely taking her into the woods to exact revenge. Despite her logic though, she wasn't getting that hair-raising feeling she got when something was going south.

"You should know," she said as she slid into the passenger seat, "I am trained in self-defense."

"Yeah, I could tell by the way you went limp the other day when I charged."

"I shot you first, smartass."

Kirk let off a single, "Ha!" But then looked surprised that he'd laughed. He turned the engine, and it roared to life.

The seats smelled like rich leather, and he had an air freshener that read *new car smell* along the bottom. It hung from the rearview mirror, swaying back and forth as he pulled out of her circle drive. The Mustang was a manual transmission, so he shifted expertly and gassed it onto the main road. The unexpected speed tickled her stomach.

Kirk looked at her quick, his eyes on her smiling lips, before he dragged his attention back to the road. "Chicks dig the car," he said.

"Oh, my God, you're one of those guys," she said, leaning back against the headrest.

"What kind of guys?"

"You know." She narrowed her eyes and repeated, "You *know*."

"Okay, cop, spill it. Tell me what kind of guy I am, based on your two seconds of talking to me."

She sighed and stretched her legs out. "You're cocky. Sexy and you know it. Drive the car for attention and because the shifter groupies in town drop their panties when you drive by with that rumbling motor. You're a vroom vroom get-em-wet guy. You've probably banged thirty women in the back seat and at least five against the hood because that's part of the bad boy lure. I bet I can guess what will come on the stereo if I turn it on. It'll be something older and rocky with a hard-hitting beat. And you're a one-chance kind of man."

"What the hell does that even mean?"

"If I put my bare feet on your glove box, breathed on your window, smudged your leather, or brought a drink in here, you would never let me ride in your car again."

"Sexy and I know it," he said, shooting her a quick grin.

"That's what you took away from all that?"

"Well, it's the only part that's true. I thought a cop would be better at this, but clearly—"

"Tell me which parts are wrong," she challenged him.

Kirk clamped his teeth closed and shook his head. "Nah, I'm not playing this anymore. You nailed me. One hundred percent correct. Good job."

He shifted gears and hit the gas, then shifted up again. Her stomach dipped with the speed, and she let off a surprised laugh. Kirk grinned and hit another gear, and now they were flying.

"You gonna give me a speeding ticket?"

"Yes!" she said giggling as she held her stomach. It was like being on a roller coaster. "Slow down right now."

The engine wailed as he let off the gas and downshifted. "Yes, ma'am."

He hit the blinker and turned onto a dirt road, but they'd already passed the turnoff for the Grayland Mobile Park.

"Where are you taking me? Damon is a Gray Back."

"False. Damon is whatever he wants to be. He has pledged to no one, and neither has his mate or son."

"Why not?"

Kirk shot her a nice-try look. "If you have questions about the dragon, you can ask him yourself and see how much he tells you. I like my hide where it is, thank you very much."

"You mean you don't want to be burned and eaten."

"Damon wouldn't do that," Kirk said quietly.

"Why not?"

"Because he'd never hurt the people he loves. You think he's a monster, but he's lived for millennia and has seen the real beasts. And they aren't you or me. It's good to be wary of the dragon. He deserves respect. But he's also a good man, and one worth getting to know."

"Why are you helping me?"

Kirk twitched his head and made a single click behind his teeth. He pulled onto another road and sped along the gravel, kicking up clouds of dust. "I don't know why I'm helping."

"Lie," she bluffed.

Kirk shifted gears again and inhaled deeply, his chest rising with the motion. "Because I can't stop thinking about..."

Her heart pounded against her sternum. "Can't stop thinking about what?"

"How you looked that first night, when you were giving us the news that laws for shifters were changing. We're having our rights stripped away, and Brackeen didn't give a single fuck how that affected us, but you looked at Bash and Emerson, and you were gutted with us. Do you know other shifters?"

"No. You're the first ones I've met."

"And yet you know how to expose your neck when we're riled up. You know not to give us your back and run. Bringing the gun was dumb as shit, but everything else, you got. I'm helping because maybe if you see how life really is up here, you won't be scared of us. You won't go back to your boss and tell them what animals we are. Maybe you'll see more, and maybe you'll be better for it. You want to work up in these mountains and have access to us? You won't get that pointing your Glock at everyone. We're people, Ally. We have families up here, mates, people we love. How would you like if someone came into your home and pointed a gun at the people you love?"

Ally blinked hard and stared out the window so he couldn't see the loss in her eyes when she said, "I do know how that feels."

Kirk was quiet for a while, and they drove deeper into the mountains in silence. At last he said, "I'm sorry for whatever you've gone through, but can you see why we get defensive? We've been through more than you can imagine, just fighting for normal."

Alison sighed and reached forward, turned the volume up on the radio. A rap song came on. Not many people surprised her, and Kirk was proving to be a breath of fresh air.

"The car wasn't to get pubby," he said. "My dad gave it to me. He gave one to all his kids to fix up."

"How many kids did he have?"

Kirk's lips turned up in a vacant smile. "You'll judge."

"I won't. Tell me."

"Fifteen."

"Fifteen kids?" she said way too loud.

"Told you."

"No, no, I'm not judging," she rasped out, trying to regain her composure. "Your mother must've loved being pregnant."

"Mothers. I lived in a family group. Gorilla shifters are different. One silverback for several females. At least we were different until Kong upended our entire society. Now it's a free-for-all. My people are scrambling to figure out whether to continue in their family groups or pair up with a single mate."

"And you? What have you decided?" She hoped he wanted a single mate.

"No."

"No, what?"

"We're not getting into *feeling* shit. You shot me. You're dangerous to my people, and I'm not bonding with you. I want a hundred mates. I want to fuck every woman I meet, and I want them all to be mine." His voice had gone hollow and strange sounding. "I'll never settle down with one. I'm a big dominant breeder, and I'll be just as aloof to the tens of kids I father as my dad was with me. Don't ask me questions like that anymore."

He pulled up to the side of a cliff where a construction crew was working to rebuild a demolished house right into the rocky face. She wanted to be awed, but she was having trouble keeping her gaze from Kirk for too long.

"What's your problem?" she asked. She'd never been a fan of men who were hot and cold, and Kirk was the ice king right now.

"Rebellious teenager," Kirk guessed. "You wanted to be a cop to feel powerful. Submissive personality you hate, so you picked a job where you could bully people and feel empowered. No friends because you give up on people to avoid rejection. You pull triggers easily because you're scared, and then you feel guilt because you realize you've lost the person you wanted to be." He dragged his dark gaze to her. "How close am I?"

She huffed a disgusted sound and shook her head, infinitely disappointed in what a jerk he'd turned out to be. Her eyes burned as she said, "Rebellious teenager, check. Raised in a girls' home, no parents, landed in juvie three times before I got recruited right out of high school."

His face went slack. "Recruited for what?"

"Undercover narcotics. And I don't have friends because *fuck you*." She threw him one last dirty look and shoved the door open. "I can find my way back without your help." She slammed his door and walked toward the half-built house.

Alison shook her head and blinked her

eyes hard because he didn't deserve this emotional reaction from her. He was a complete stranger, and not a nice one like she'd thought. His engine roared, and gravel sprayed behind her as he spun out and drove away.

Good riddance.

She would rather walk all the way back to her cabin than sit in the car another minute with Kirk Slater.

# FOUR

Alison stopped at a massive burn mark across the lawn. It probably stretched the length of an acre, and suddenly, she regretted telling her only safety net to piss off. Even if Kirk had been a jerk, he'd sounded sincere when he'd said he wouldn't let anything happen to her. But now, she was standing right in front of the dragon's lair, weaponless, and probably smelling like dinner.

"You smell scared," a deep voice said from the trees.

Alison jumped and instinctively reached for a gun that wasn't at her hip.

Damon Daye stepped out of the shadows of the woods. He wore a fine, charcoal-gray suit, and his dark hair was mussed on top. It was a youthful cut that contrasted with the first hints of silver at his temples. His dark eyes were hard as stone. He looked unassuming enough, and dashing even, but his presence pressed a weight upon her shoulders she'd only felt once before, the night she was trying to save Emerson Elliot from the clutches of the Boarlanders who had apparently not kidnapped her like her faulty intel had stated.

Damon housed the biggest and most dangerous monster of all.

Alison straightened her spine and cleared her throat. "I asked for a meeting with you two weeks ago."

"And I denied it. Ms. Holman, you do realize this is private property, do you not? Without a warrant or probable cause to be here, I don't have to answer any of your questions. Now, your first impression left much to be desired. I don't enjoy seeing weapons pointed at my friends. It makes me feel…" A low, prehistoric rumble sounded from the man, and his eyes lightened to a terrifying silver color. "Angry," he finished.

Holy shit, Damon was scary. She cleared her throat, stalling so that her voice wouldn't tremble when she spoke. "Then why now? Why have you finally decided to meet with me after all this time?"

"Because you have a champion in your corner."

"Who?"

"Kirk Slater."

Well, that drew her up short. "But...he hates me."

Damon lifted his chin and placed his hands formally behind his back. He narrowed his eyes slightly. "Hate is a strong word, and not what he feels, I think. You have this meeting because he reminded me of the favor you did for some of the people I care about."

"What favor?"

"When you delivered the news that the laws concerning shifters were changing, you went against your partner to give Emerson that note. *Call Cora Keller.* You knew Emerson might be able to sneak her marriage to Bash under the wire if she had the right information. And you, for whatever reason, gave us that information. I'm intrigued by you, Alison Holman. You surprised me, and I assure you, I'm not surprised easily."

Most likely a product of his immortality. Or what *was* his immortality, because rumor had it, the dragon was mortal now.

"Why are you here?"

Damon's sudden, direct question caught

40

her off guard, so she stumbled on the answer. "Uuuh, to serve as the point of contact—"

"Between the outside world and my mountains, yes, yes, you said that when I met you the first time. Now chip away at the bullshit and tell me what is really happening."

"I'm not entirely sure."

Damon frowned and cocked his head. His eyes were still silver, but now his pupils were slowly elongating. "Explain."

"My partner and I were chosen for a special task force, but we weren't told what it was until right before we got on a plane headed for Wyoming. We learned about the last minute changes to shifter rights on our way here. My guess is they're worried about retaliation from you and from your people."

"My friends, not my people."

"Saratoga has a police force, but way up here, there is no enforcement. Finn and I are now that enforcement."

"Have you been asked to watch us? To report on our behavior?"

"No. Which is surprising because that would make more sense. My job description is to ensure you abide by the laws and to keep humans, especially human women, from making their way into your mountains."

"Why?"

"Because they don't want any more dragons. They didn't tell me that specifically, but it's the only thing that makes sense."

"I'm not building an army, you know. I'm building a family."

She swallowed and dropped her gaze. "It wasn't my choice for them to start stripping rights. If there had been a vote, I would've voted against it."

"You're pro-shifter?"

"Apparently so."

Damon became quiet and watched her for a long time before he said, "Follow me, Alison Holman."

"You can call me Ally." She followed behind him as he stepped gingerly over the lean taper of a burn mark on the earth.

"I did my research on you too, Ally."

Dread dumped into her stomach. "What do you mean?"

"That's what you do, right? You have access to personal information on anyone you suspect is doing wrong?" Touché. "I know what happened in Chicago. I know where you came from, which is why you've surprised me. You should've turned hard. You should've gone dark, but you gave Emerson that note. It must be a lonely life, living undercover. Never being able to trust anyone or open up. Always pretending to be someone you aren't." Damon shot her a significant look. "That's how it is to be a shifter. Or it was before the government required us to register. Hiding kept us alive."

Alison's heart was pounding so hard against her chest, her entire torso ached. She pushed aside a clump of plants that covered the trail and sidled past them. "I don't like to talk about Chicago."

"The point, Ally, is that bone-deep loneliness you must have felt? I know all about that. I've lived a long time, and at some point, after I'd watched everyone die and everything change, I shut down."

Alison shook her head and resisted the urge to double over the pain in her middle. "You've lost a lot?"

"More than you can imagine. And then this happened." Damon stepped through a final line of trees and onto the bank near a waterfall. He gestured to a red-headed woman in the river, holding a little boy, who was clutching onto her shoulders and giggling as she spun them fast. The little boy had a crop of curly red hair, like his momma's, but his eyes were dark like Damon's. "That right there makes up most of my world now. Clara and I didn't have a baby to build some line of defense, Ally. We had a child because she wanted to be a mother, and I wanted to be a father again. A good father this time."

"Is he a dragon?"

Damon blinked slowly and leveled her with a hollow look. "Does it matter?"

"To the world, it will."

"To me it doesn't. To me, I care about him growing up safe. I care about him being happy. I care about my mate not staying up at nights worrying about his future or his right to choose his own mate."

Alison leaned back against a tree and watched Clara laugh and lay smacking kisses all over the child's face until he scrunched up his shoulders and laughed. "Can I ask you a question?"

"You may." *But I reserve the right to answer or not.* That last part wasn't said out loud, but it didn't have to be. His tone implied enough.

"How did you do it?"

Damon angled his face to her, but his eyes stayed on his mate and child. "Do what?"

She lowered her voice to a whisper. "How did you let them in?"

If he'd known true loneliness, he would

44

understand her question. How did he open up his heart to something as dangerous as love?

"It took a long time, but eventually I had to take the risk to care again or lose everything good about myself." He arced his darkening gaze to hers. "Ally, you have one short lifetime. Choose where to take a stand before it's too late."

"Everyone I've ever cared about has gotten hurt."

Damon inhaled deeply. "Then get better at protecting them. You have my permission to come onto my land, but your partner does not. He doesn't care about the people here, and he stinks of anti-shifter. We have children up here. Families to protect. You will be safe, but he will push too far. For our safety and his, Finn Brackeen needs to stay off my land unless he has an actual reason to be up here. I will cooperate with you, but you'll be escorted by Kirk."

"Kirk? But he has better things to do than—"

"You shot one of my friends, Alison Holman." He arched his dark eyebrows and dared her to deny it. "I know what happens in my mountains, and Kirk has decided you deserve a second chance. I trust him and his judgement, and I'm willing to give you a chance because he's asked that of me. That gorilla hasn't ever asked anyone for anything. Take care with him. He's having a hard time, and the second I think you're making it worse for him, you will be banished from these mountains, just like Finn, and no law enforcement badge will change that. Are we clear?"

Clear as mud. She didn't understand all the riddles about Kirk. What was he having a hard time with? And why the hell would he ask a favor of the dragon for her? Damon didn't seem to want to discuss it further, though, so she nodded once, exposed her neck, and said, "Yes. We're clear."

And as Damon escorted her back through the woods, it dawned on her that this meeting hadn't clarified anything.

It had only made her more confused about her role here and these secretive people who lived in Damon's trailer parks. And most of all, she was baffled by the mysteries surrounding Kirk.

He felt important, but for the life of her, she couldn't figure out why.

# FIVE

Kirk got halfway down Damon's drive when he slammed on his brakes and skidded to a stop. Why had he done that? Getting close to Ally had caused him to push her away hard. Everything in him wanted to get to know her better, but the more he learned, the more he felt like running. She felt dangerous. Not physically, but inside of him, deep in his chest. She had the power to rile him up, and that was a problem for him, as well as her.

But as much as he wanted to escape the drugged sensation she gave him, he couldn't leave her to walk home and, sure as shit, Damon wasn't going to get her there safely. The only reason he was meeting with her was because Kirk had asked.

And now he was sitting here going over their conversation in his mind and wondering why his emotions were swinging so wide around her.

Okay, he was pissed, but why? Sure she'd pegged him all wrong and assumed he was just some asshole chasing women, but he'd pegged her wrong, too. So wrong. An orphan, raised in a girls' home, getting into trouble, and all those damned tattoos made more sense now. He wondered if she got them before or after spending time undercover. Narcotics? Holy fuck, she had seen things. Probably awful things, and now it dawned on him that she was confusing his senses because maybe she was broken.

Just like him.

"Fuck," he yelled, slamming his hand against the steering wheel. He should run. He should've never begged her a meeting with Damon or gotten involved at all. He should've left her alone, but she was so damned intriguing. His animal had been a beast to deal with since she'd shot him.

And what did that say about him? Every time he thought about her, or spent time around her, his inner animal drew up and pined to be closer to the woman who'd blasted a bullet into his shoulder. For fuck's sake, he was even more messed up than he'd realized.

He should go back to the Lowlanders down in Saratoga and far away from Alison Holman. Ally. She'd given him permission to use a name she liked. A name for friends, and what had he done? Got desperate, got scared, got mean. Typical Kirk. That's exactly why Fiona hadn't trusted him to run a family group. That's why she had assigned him to guard Kong and ready him to head a family group instead. Kong was always the better option.

No, it wasn't right for him to get jealous. Kong had never asked for that kind of treatment and, hell, if anyone was in the wrong, it was Kirk for accepting a bodyguard position. He'd kept Kong miserable for years. He fucking deserved to have an interesting, beautiful woman dangled in front of his face, only to realize she was broken. He wasn't the kind of man who could fix anyone. He was shit mate material, and Ally would be better off without him complicating her life.

But, damn it all, "complicated" was so tempting right now.

The way she'd said "Fuck you" had given him a massive boner that was still at full mast, even though he was still pissed at himself, at fate. *Of course* his gorilla would choose an unattainable, messed up mate who had seen too much grit to ever really know how to love. *Of course* he would pick a mate two fuckin' weeks after human-shifter pairings were declared illegal. He wanted to laugh and scream and break everything. More proof he was losing his mind.

But no matter how hard his feelings were churning, Ally still needed an escort out of these mountains. Not because he thought the crews were dangerous to her, but because he didn't want her getting lost or stumbling onto some unknown danger in the wild woods of Damon's mountains. Yeah, see? Add overprotective to the list of disastrous traits his gorilla had adopted since he'd seen her that first night.

He pulled a U-turn and drove back up to Damon's half-finished mansion and came to a stop before the clearing because, dammit, he had to play this cool. He couldn't seem like an overeager puppy with a lady like Ally. She was flighty. Her career said as much. He bet she could shut down on people the second she wanted to.

Kirk cut the engine and relaxed back against the seat, waiting to see her again.

Ten minutes later, Ally crested a mound of scorched earth, her frown directed at the ashes around her feet. He couldn't give much of himself, but he could give her an explanation on what had happened to Damon's lair. But then again, he had to be careful with the information he offered. She was here for a reason, and one he didn't understand or like, and if she was here to spy on the shifters, he had to make sure she was trustworthy before he gave her anything.

She wore light-wash jeans that hugged her hips and thighs. She'd worn her uniform the first night she'd tried to save Emerson, but she seemed much more comfortable in the jeans and figure-hugging black cotton shirt she wore. Her shirt had bunched behind the gold badge that glinted from the waist of her jeans, showing a tiny patch of fair skin on her stomach. Fuck, his fingers itched to touch her there. Ally probably hadn't had much use for a uniform before if she'd worked undercover.

She cast a worried glance behind her, then crossed her arms over her chest, as if she had caught a chill. Good instincts. Damon had that effect on people.

Kirk turned on the engine, and Ally looked up, her crystal blue eyes startled. She slowed and ran her fingers through her bleach-blond hair, pushing it back from her face. With another quick look back behind her, she made her way slowly to his car.

Kirk rolled down the window, and she leaned her elbows against the open frame, giving him one hell of a view of those tiny, perky tits under that V-neck. Black bra to match her shirt and, holy fuck, he hoped her panties matched.

"Tell me why you got me a meeting with Damon. And try to do it without staring at my boobs."

Kirk tried and failed to drag his gaze from her chest. "Lady, if you want answers, you'll have to put them away."

With an irritated sigh, Ally yanked open the door and slid into the seat. "You feel heavy, and the air in here is too thick to breathe."

Kirk rolled down his window too to try and thin out the air. "I was pissed."

"At me?" she asked softly.

"No. At me. I didn't mean to hurt you."

Her big blue gaze collided with his. In a voice barely higher than a whisper, she admitted, "I didn't mean to hurt you either. I shouldn't have judged. I forget I'm not the only one with baggage sometimes, you know?"

Kirk lifted his hips, adjusted his dick, and offered her an unapologetic smile. "You're not my type. I like curvy women with big tits and asses. Brunettes with long hair."

Rude but not that surprising. She didn't exactly have men beating down her door. "Kirk, do you want to know one of the big reasons I was recruited when I was so young?"

"Why?"

"Because I'm naturally rail-thin. They needed a small girl, someone who looked weak and strung-out. A girl who looked like a druggie, but without an addiction." Sadness washed through her eyes. "The things you hate were exactly what someone else was looking for in a woman."

"You mean what a handler was looking for, not a man who was supposed to enjoy your body."

Ally clenched that sexy pixie jaw of hers and smelled like anger.

Shaking her head, she shoved open the door and got halfway out before he said, "Don't run. Just listen to what I have to say. You asked me why I got you the meeting. I'll tell you."

Ally stood frozen, half out of his car. He thought she would still leave, but she sat on the edge of the seat and offered him a look over her shoulder instead. "I'm listening."

"What I was trying to say is you aren't my usual type"—he jammed his finger at his hard-on—"so this makes no damned sense to me. Suddenly, nobody is pretty to me anymore. No one unless they have short blond hair, tiny, kissable lips, big blue eyes, and the frame of a waif. Small, perky tits are apparently my thing now. And tattoos. Fuck, Ally, I can't tell you how many times I've tried to imagine where your tattoos end. I got you a meeting because you asked Damon for it that first night, and I knew he was putting you off. I got you the meeting because I can't—" He shook his head. It was too much, too fast.

"Finish it."

Kirk swallowed hard and gripped the steering wheel until the leather creaked under his choking grasp. "Because I'm having trouble getting you out of my head. You wanted something, and it made me feel good to get it for you. I got you the meeting because even though I know you'll bring me trouble, I like you."

Ally let off a long, shaking sigh, and she leaned back against the headrest and closed her eyes. "Can you say that last part again?"

He studied her profile. Something about her face had relaxed, and in hopes he had caused that, he murmured, "I like you."

She winced, and her shoulders drew up to her ears, and when she looked back at him, her eyes were rimmed with moisture. He didn't understand her tears, so he reached forward and brushed the pad of his thumb under her eye, catching the drop of moisture before it streamed down her cheek.

"Why?" he whispered.

"Because it feels so damned good to hear something nice. It feels good to be liked."

And he got it. He'd grown up in a family group with focus on breeding for numbers, not child-rearing. She'd grown up without parents. Grown up with strangers, and then she'd gone undercover where likely she hadn't been allowed to love or receive love in return. Dangerous little broken bird. His inner gorilla was practically beating his chest with an oath to keep her safe from hurt.

Kirk pulled his car in a slow circle, following a scorch mark where grass was still determined not to grow.

"What happened here?" Ally asked, her eyes on the destroyed mansion.

Kirk had to fight hard against the need to touch her. Ally's hands were resting on her thighs, and every instinct in his body screamed to wrap her hand in his. Shaking his head hard, he explained, "Damon wasn't the only immortal dragon left after the dragon wars. He had an enemy, a dark dragon. One who had been badly burned by Damon's fire and who had built his strength up over centuries to take him on again."

"So he destroyed this place out of revenge?" Ally asked.

"Partly. Marcus also wanted to rule the whole damned world, and the only thing that could stop him was Damon."

"Where is Marcus now?"

"Dead. The good dragon won."

"The good dragon," she murmured.

"Yes, Ally." Kirk shot her a glance, then dragged his eyes back to the gravel road disappearing under his tires. "Damon is good. He sacrificed a lot through the centuries to keep the world safe. More than anyone will ever know. The government fears him, but without him, none of us would be here. And I don't just mean shifters. I mean *none* of us."

# SIX

Alison had about a billion things to think about now. Everything Brackeen had constantly ranted about the past two weeks was wrong. It was feelings of anger and fear he'd adopted from outside sources, not an actual personal opinion garnered from time spent with the shifters.

Kirk pulled to a stop in front of her small cabin and put the car in park. "You asked me a question earlier, and I got angry and retaliated by saying things that weren't true."

"About wanting a hundred mates?"

His lips curved into a slow smile. "Yeah. That's not how I feel. I used to want a family group. I wanted to be responsible for the protection of any females I was worthy enough to have placed in my group. But then my friend Kong picked a single mate, and something clicked with me. I started wanting that instead." He ducked his gaze to the steering wheel, and his hair fell in front of his face. "I *want* that. My animal wants it, too."

Her heart was pounding fast. Wearing a slight frown, he cast her chest a glance as if he could hear it. Hell, maybe he could.

"Look, I get it. This is a lot and it's fast, and just forget it. This ain't a come-on. It's just me feeling bad for a lie and coming clean. I'll see you around, Alison."

She grimaced at the use of her full name, but okay. He was distancing her again. She didn't like it, but she understood. She did the same thing all the time. Hot and cold was her specialty, and apparently she and Kirk had been formed from the same misshapen mold.

She got out and shut the door. "Hold on," she rushed out before he drove away. Ally gripped the open window frame and leaned down. "Damon said I can only go onto his land if you escort me."

Kirk narrowed his eyes and gripped the stick shift. "Hmm."

"I told him you have better things to do, but that was the rule he laid down, and I don't want to be dragon food."

"I work all day up on the jobsite. I'm a

logger, so it's pretty much from dawn to dusk most days, especially with the season ending in a couple weeks. We're slammed right now. I got today off as a favor from Harrison. Here, give me your phone." He held out his large, calloused hand. Long fingers, and damn he could probably make her feel like magic with them. "Ally?"

"What?" she rushed out, busted. "Oh, right. My phone." As she was fumbling it out of her back pocket, she dropped it on the gravel. With a muttered curse, she picked it up and shoved it through the window. And now Kirk had an obnoxiously wicked grin on his face.

Kirk's nostrils flared slightly. "You smell like you want to fool around with me."

"You stop right now. You shouldn't talk to me like that."

"Why not?"

"Because…" Well, why the hell not? There hadn't been any rules stated that she couldn't talk dirty with one of the shifters. She wasn't undercover anymore and could spend time with whoever she wanted as long as they didn't interfere with the job.

"Ally, I would break you. My appetite is too big for a woman like you."

She made an offended snort. "Like me?

What the hell does that mean?"

"I mean you don't want anything to do with a big rutting gorilla shifter. I'm not gentle, and you need that. We might get along fine, but you and I wouldn't be compatible in the bedroom."

"And you just know this? Not like I'm arguing for you to sleep with me, but I'm a little irritated you're being the judgmental one now. I'm stronger than I look."

"Yeah? And when I lose control and bite you? When I lose my mind mid-fuck and give you a claiming mark that is illegal now, what will you do? Your job? Will you arrest me or keep my mark a secret? I want you bad, Ally. It don't mean I can have you, though."

Kirk tapped a number and saved it her phone, then shoved it toward her. "Show me where your tattoo ends."

Surprised, Ally laughed and stood back. "No one sees that part of me."

Kirk lifted his chin, his eyes dancing. He rested his wrist over his steering wheel, a picture of confident, cocky male. "I've banged zero girls in the back of my ride and zero girls against the hood. You were wrong. Now it's your turn to share. Let me see."

Ally's cheeks heated, and she looked

around to see if Brackeen's cruiser was parked in front of his cabin. Nope. No one here but her and Kirk, the sexy, pervy gorilla shifter. She hadn't gotten the tattoos for sex appeal, but Kirk didn't seem to care about that. He liked them. Liked her.

Feeling reckless, she turned and lifted the back of her shirt an inch, exposing just a sliver of ink. It didn't tell him where they ended, but it told him they hadn't ended at her arm.

Behind her, Kirk murmured, "Fuuuck, that's sexy."

With a cheeky grin over her shoulder, she sauntered to the door of her cabin. And before she disappeared inside, she told him, "You couldn't break me if you tried."

Feeling particularly amused with herself, she giggled privately and swung the door closed. Only before it clicked into place, a big dusty work boot had wedged into the frame. Whoa, Kirk was fast. When he pushed open the door, his eyes weren't the dark brown they'd been in the car. They were glowing an intense gold as he stalked forward and closed the door behind him, preventing her escape with his inhuman gaze.

He gripped the back of her neck, and his lips twisted into a devilish smile. She thought his kiss would be violent, but when his mouth pressed to hers, he surprised her to stillness with how soft his lips were. She was melting into the floor. Her knees were buckling, struggling to hold her upright, so she clutched onto the front of his shirt and hoped it would be enough. Kirk angled his head and pushed his tongue past her lips, filling her, tasting her. Slowly, he turned them and eased her back to the wall, and the second her shoulder blades touched the solid surface, he ground his hips against hers.

The needy moan in her throat couldn't be helped. Not when his erection was so hard, so thick, hitting her just right. His fingers brushed her skin at her hip, right above her jeans and under her shirt, and with a jerk of his muscles, he threw her badge on the ground. "Now your off-duty," he murmured against her lips with a smile. Then he slid his hand under her shirt and brushed his fingertips up her ribs until he reached her bra.

"What color are your panties," he asked in a low, growly voice that sent delicious shivers up her spine.

She didn't want this moment to stop. She was having a genuine physical and emotional connection with someone for the first time in years. Maybe the first time ever, and she didn't want to waste it. She wanted to be brave like Damon had been and open herself up to someone. "See for yourself," she challenged him.

The snap of her jeans popped open as Kirk kissed her, and then his lips left hers just long enough for him to shove her pants down.

He cupped her cheeks and searched her eyes as he pressed his pelvis against hers. A needy sound left her lips at how good he felt. Chest heaving, Kirk eased back and dragged his hungry gaze down her body. A satisfied smile took his face when he laid eyes on her black, lacey panties. Kirk was a lingerie man. Good to know.

With a languid blink, he lifted his gold eyes back to hers. He kissed her again, slower this time, then trailed soft, biting kisses down her jaw and along her neck until his lips were right next to her ear. "You aren't ready for all of me, woman, no matter what you say. But you'll fuck my hand, and it'll be enough for now. You'll think about me when you touch yourself tonight, and you'll call me in the morning, making up some excuse to get an escort onto Damon's land just to see me again."

Cocky. She wanted to deny him, but

confidence was the sexiest thing about a man and now her panties were slowly soaking just thinking about coming on his hand.

"Beg me," he murmured, then pulled her earlobe gently between his teeth. He ran his hand from her bra slowly down her belly, then hooked his fingers just under the band of her panties. So close. "Do it. Beg me."

She was soaking wet now and desperate for him to fulfill those pretty promises. Kirk would be able to make her come. She just knew he could.

"Please," she asked in a needier whisper than she'd intended. "Touch me."

Kirk tensed his arm as he slid a gentle touch down the front of her panties. He dragged his fingertip down her wet sex and, curiously, he shuddered. "Perfect," he whispered as she rolled her hips toward him.

She rested her head back against the wall and gasped as he dipped his finger inside of her. "Kirk," she whispered, hooking her fingers on the waist of his jeans. She wanted to feel him, too.

Her entire body was shaking with how good his touch felt. She should be embarrassed by how wet she was, but Kirk seemed to love it, and he was kissing her again, his tongue dipping into her mouth each time he pushed his finger into her.

Desperate for more, she pressed her hand farther down the front of his jeans until her fingers brushed the hard, swollen head of his cock. So big. She wished she could see it. He moaned a sexy, vibrating noise as he bucked his hips against her. Mindlessly, she unbuttoned the snap and ripped his zipper downward. Without the barrier, she could run her hand up the length of him. Huge dick to match the rest of his massive body, and now she got it. Maybe she *couldn't* take size like this.

When Kirk slid a second finger in her the next time, she gasped and bowed against him. He was hitting her clit just right. Ally pulled the length of him slowly, from the base up, and he let off a low, rattling growl. Sensitive man, writhing under her touch. She'd never affected anyone like this. Power like this was addictive. She rolled her hips with his touch and matched the pace he set by stroking him in rhythm. So much pressure was building up inside of her, and with each push into her, she became desperate for more. For release.

She was losing control, and her hips weren't moving as smoothly anymore. She was twitching with need under his touch, kissing him harder, biting his bottom lip, a helpless moan in her throat.

Kirk's body was tense, hard, and strung tighter than a bowstring. In a rush, he settled her back on the floor so fast the room spun. Yes! He was losing control and giving in, and she reveled in the fact that she was the reason. Kirk was as helpless in this moment as she was. She wasn't alone in this need for connection. She kicked her jeans off her ankles and bent her knees, creating a cradle for him to settle into between her thighs.

"Ally," he gritted out. "It's hard to stop."

"I'm on birth control," she whispered.

"Fuck, woman, not helping." His hips bucked as she pulled another firm stroke of his dick.

She could see it now and geez, she'd never seen anything more masculine and powerful than his shaft sticking out rigid between his powerful legs. His hand cupped her sex again, and she rocked against his palm, closing her eyes at how good he felt. They were so damned close, but not close enough. Kirk shoved her shirt up her stomach. "I'm gonna come on you," he murmured. "Soon," he gritted out, pumping his hips.

Her, too. She was on the edge, nearly blinded with ecstasy.

"More, more, more, Kirk. Please!"

"Ally, don't ask, or I won't be able to stop."

She answered by pulling the head of his shaft against the wetness he'd conjured between her legs. His movement slowed, became smoother as he let off another sexy growl. He rolled his striking gold eyes closed and eased down closer to her, his triceps flexing where his arms were locked on either side of her face.

"I want all of you," she whispered, pushing his tip against her entrance.

His rocking motion was so graceful he didn't miss a beat when she pulled his shirt over his head just to watch his abs flex above her. Ally was stunned at his masculine beauty as he lowered to his forearms. His dick looked perfect in her hand, pushing through the circle she'd made, and she imagined him inside of her working them both toward release.

Kirk's brows were furrowed with intensity, and he huffed a breath as she brought his tip against her again. He leaned down and kissed her as he pushed his head into her and eased back out. Gently, he pulled her hand away from him and slid into her again, deeper.

"I won't last long. I'm close," he murmured against her lips. "Fuck, Ally. You feel so good around me."

She spread her legs wider and rolled her hips, meeting him blow for blow. So wet. So easy, like they'd been made to fit together. Kirk's pace became erratic, and he bucked into her faster, harder. She called out as her orgasm coursed through her, gripping his dick in deep pulses. Kirk's body went rigid against her as he gritted out her name. His cock pulsed deliciously, and warmth filled her. Wrapping his arm around her back, he stroked into her faster, hesitating every time he spilled more seed into her. And when he was emptied and her after shocks slowed, she relaxed under him and smiled. She was glowing. She had to be. That's the only thing that would explain this incredible feeling inside of her.

With a shake of his head, Kirk grinned. "Temptress."

"I told you you wouldn't break me."

"I was careful on purpose."

"Mmm hmm," she said, disbelieving. "Or I'm a stronger bedmate than you'd expected."

"Bedmate," he murmured, pushing her short hair from her forehead. His eyes were still blazing that inhuman color, but they softened as he searched her face. "You're trouble for me and my people, Ally, but I'm in this now. Don't hurt us."

Unable to speak at witnessing such raw desperation in his eyes, she pulled his wrist to her lips and kissed him in a gentle promise that she would take care of him.

He was so wrong.

She had no power to hurt him or his people. Her heart wouldn't allow it.

But Kirk Slater now had the complete ability to drag her to her knees and cut her deeply.

# SEVEN

There was a knock on the door, but hell if Kirk wanted to talk to anyone. "Piss off, Clinton."

When the door swung wide, Kirk lifted his attention from pulling his muddy boots off long enough to grace Mason with an irritated look. "You here to rag on me, too? I said I was sorry."

Mason made his way past on a direct course for the fridge. "No, you didn't. You said, and I quote, 'Fuck all of you. If you get stuck in a mudslide, it would shut y'all the hell up, and I could get a minute of peace.'"

"It was close to an apology," Kirk muttered, leaving his boots in a pile by the couch and stomping into the kitchen to grab some paper towels.

The refrigerator light illuminated Mason's

troubled expression and suntanned face. "Where was your head at today, man? You could've got us killed with how reckless you were cutting those trees above us."

Kirk gritted his teeth and pushed off the counter, then began wiping thick mud off the soles of his boots. "What are you gonna do?"

"About what?" Mason pulled a beer out of the fridge and popped the top.

"Pick up the cap, asshole."

Mason snorted and kicked the bottle cap under the table, then gave him a *fuck-you* glare and sank down onto the couch beside him.

"I mean, what are you gonna do when logging season is over?" Kirk mumbled.

Mason frowned at him but kept chugging his beer. With a satisfied sigh, he wiped his mouth and said, "Is that what has your panties in a twist? The end of logging season? Brother, this was always temporary. We're just hired help for the season. Harrison's already looking at applications for October."

Kirk hated the way that made him feel. Expendable. Replaceable. It hurt in ways he hadn't expected.

"You ever think of settling down?" he asked Mason.

"All the damned time. It's impossible not

to, right? The Gray Backs are all paired up. My best friend started a family."

"Damon did move on quick, didn't he?"

Mason chuckled. "No. It took him centuries, and I'm happy he found Clara, but seeing everyone so happy makes me want things I won't find."

"So, when Damon finishes rebuilding his house, will you go back with him? Will you be his driver and assistant again?"

"Shit, I don't know." Mason relaxed against the couch cushion and picked at the label on his beer bottle. "I've been thinking about it, but I don't know where I belong anymore. I never pledged to anyone."

"Why didn't you pick a crew?"

"Because bear people don't work like that. We stick with our own kind. The second I register, they would come after me and yank me back to fulfill my duties. I'm happy-ish in these mountains."

"Happy-ish?"

"Yeah, man. Don't pretend you don't feel the ache. Feel the burn of the outside. You're one of the last singles, too. What about you. What's the plan, Lowlander?"

Kirk shook his head and set his semi-clean boot down, then started on the other. "Don't call me that."

"Why not? There are worse alphas to put yourself under besides Kong."

"Yeah, well, Kong isn't an alpha. My gorilla-people don't work like that. One silverback per family group. He's got my animal stifled, and my instincts right along with them. I have my eyes on a female. A woman," he corrected himself, because Ally wasn't just some gorilla female ready to breed. She was more. Everything, maybe.

Mason sat straight up. "Who?"

"Officer Holman," he said through a smirk.

"Dancin' with the devil, are you?"

"Don't call her that."

"She isn't one of us, and she isn't just some human, Kirk. She's one of them. She's the first wind of the tornado headed our way, and you're holding your arms out, waiting for her to carry you away. Careful with that one."

"I thought you'd understand."

Mason glared at him a half a minute too long. "Have you told Harrison?"

"Nope. Just you."

Mason cursed and stretched out one of his legs, then sighed. "Do you trust her?"

"Yeah, but it's different for you and me now, Mason. We have nothing to offer a human woman anymore. Nothing can legally bind us to them."

"Until they reinstate our rights."

"And how long with that take? How long do you think?"

Mason looked tired and shrugged one shoulder up. "I don't know, man."

Kirk didn't either, but he did understand the answer to that question could be *never*. Kirk was prepared to be patient and wait on that slow human timeline until Ally was ready to settle down, but then what? What commitment could he possibly give her that would mean anything? He couldn't claim her by shifter laws, and he couldn't marry her by human ones. They'd have to carry on, just like this, until the government got tired of meddling in shifter affairs.

"She was better off without me, and by a lot."

"You kissed her yet?" Mason asked quietly.

"I'm not talking to you about that."

"I'm not asking as a pervert so shut your defenses down. I've had a mate before, and I know how it feels when you lock on. Heart pounding when you even think about seeing her, wanting to taste her all the time, needing to hear her voice, your animal going nuts when it's been too long between visits, that bone-deep instinct to breed her and start a family just to tether her to you. Are you there yet?"

Kirk dropped his boot and wadded up the dirty paper towels. He stared out the open blinds to the rainy day beyond. With a sigh, he admitted, "Yeah. I'm there."

"Then ask me what you really want to."

Kirk debated not saying anything else. He wasn't into therapy hour. In fact, he'd always prided himself on being an island that no one could reach. But suddenly, he was having all these inconvenient *feelings*, and hell, maybe it wouldn't hurt to ask Mason for advice on the decision that was doubling him over. Pitching his bad moods left and right sure wasn't working. "Should I go back to Kong's Lowlanders? If he stifles my animal, maybe, in time, the instinct to settle her will lessen."

Mason huffed a humorless sound and scrubbed his hand over the three-day beard on his jaw. When he looked at Kirk again, there was sadness in Mason's eyes. "That feeling won't ever go away, Kirk. Not even if you ripped your beating heart from your chest. Kong won't save you from your mate."

"I'm not trying to save myself," Kirk

murmured, gaze following the streams of rainwater that raced down the window pane. "I'm trying to save her."

# EIGHT

Alison chewed distractedly on the end of her pen and stared out the front window at the drizzling rain outside. At this rate, it would turn her front yard into a weed swamp in no time. Her suitcase still sat packed on the floor of the single bedroom. A part of her had thought her boss would pull her back any minute when he found out how little work there was to do here.

She checked her phone, but nope. Still no calls, no texts, no response to the voicemail she'd left Kirk yesterday. This was the part she'd forgotten about—the insecurity that came after sleeping with a man.

"Read this bullshit," Finn said from his seat at the end of the desk. He shoved a newspaper across the clean surface as a tiny belch left him.

The article he pointed to was titled "My Five Hour Engagement to a Shifter" by Emerson Kane. It was a five paragraph article about how her wedding was beautiful, but it pointed out the unfairness of being rushed into it due to the shifters being stripped of their rights. Good for her.

When Alison had heard Emerson and Bash had been able to get their marriage in under the wire, she'd been so relieved. And now Emerson had her first article published in the Saratoga newspaper, front page and everything. She should send her congratulation flowers. Er...no. That wasn't appropriate because of her job. Right?

Finn was glaring. "Why do you look mushy? Please don't tell me you buy into all this pro-shifter crap." He let off another burp, and now that she was paying attention to him, he looked terrible, all watery-eyed and red-faced to match his hair.

"What's wrong with you? Why are you so sweaty?"

He wrapped his arms around his stomach and doubled over. "My stomach is eating itself. One of the shifters came by and brought those welcome cookies," he said, jamming an accusatory finger at the foil-covered paper plate on the edge of the desk.

Alison lifted the corner of the shiny covering with the end of her pen to expose an array of brightly frosted bear-shaped cookies.

"I think she laced them with laxatives." He groaned and winced as his stomach made an awful gurgling sound. "She also gave me a red plastic cup of worms and said they were her least favorite. Most of them were dead, and one of them was a roach. And she kept calling me Phlegm."

Alison snorted and coughed to cover up her laugh.

"It's Finn. I told her ten times."

"If you shit your pants in here, I'm filing a formal complaint against you."

"I hate this job," Finn muttered as he stumbled out of her cabin.

A week ago, she would've agreed with him, but the longer she spent here, the better she felt. Her therapist had always encouraged her to get out into nature, take a break from the job, and work through some of her issues, and here, she could do that. She *was* doing it. She'd even slept well the last few nights. No nightmares or anything. The one downfall to being up here? She checked her phone again. Being way too close and not close enough to

one sexy as hell, infinitely confusing Kirk
Slater.

Alison dumped the plate of cookies in the
trashcan and made her way into the bedroom.
She turned up the volume of a country song on
the old radio plugged into the wall and began
unpacking her clothes into the empty dresser
by the bed. It was a slow song, one of those
that sang to the soul, and she swayed with the
beat, twirled when she felt like it as she
unpacked. It wasn't until she put away the last
of her bras into the top drawer that she looked
up into the reflection in the mirror to see Kirk
standing in the open doorway, arms crossed,
chin lifted, and eyes dancing with amusement.

She gasped and spun. "What are you doing
here? How long have you been here? Why the
hell didn't you knock? It's rude just coming
into someone's house like this!"

"I'm here because I want to see you. I've
been here long enough to watch that sexy
dance of yours, and I didn't knock because the
sign on the door says *Office-Come On In*. I can
rip that down for you if you want. Bash is good
at painting signs. He can make one that says
*Fuck Off* for you, free of charge."

"It's been two, Kirk."

"One and a half, and I would've made it

80

eternity if I was strong enough."

"Wow."

He twitched his head toward the front door. "Come on."

"I'm not going anywhere with you."

Kirk narrowed his eyes. "Why are you making this difficult?"

"I'm not! You fucked me, and then you disappeared, and now you're back making demands? I'm not that kind of girl, *Kirk*." Kirk the Jerk—that's what she was going to start calling him in her head. Maybe out loud if she was feeling saucy enough.

"First off, I didn't *fuck you*, and you know it. What we did was more than that. Fucking is casual. You bound my animal to you, so don't pretend it's less than what it was."

Whatever that meant. "But you couldn't call me back?"

Kirk let off a low, inhuman rumble and glared out the window. "I'm leaving soon."

"Leaving where?"

"Saratoga. Logging season is almost over, and I'll be going back to work at the sawmill down there."

Slowly, Alison sank onto the edge of her bed. "You're leaving here?" *Leaving me?*

"It'll be best for you."

She huffed an angry laugh. "Who's running now?"

"Me," he said, void of emotion. "I'm running for the both of us because we're headed nowhere good, Alison. You don't even know me, and from what I know of you, I'm not the match you need. I'm not careful. I can't fix broken things. I break them worse."

"I'm not broken!" She drew back, feeling slapped by her own words. Shocked and more than a little relieved by her admission, she repeated, "I'm not broken. I was just bent."

A slow smile spread across Kirk's lips. "Good." His gaze dipped from her flannel shirt over her tank top to her jean shorts and then to her black flip flops. "You off work?"

"What work?" she asked darkly. All she'd done today was sit in the office and hope that someone came by so she could check them in before they headed into the mountains.

"I'm hungry, and I want to feed you because apparently I've lost my mind and think of stupid shit like that now. Has she eaten today? When does she take her showers? Mornings? Nights? What does she look like when she sleeps? Did she bring warm enough clothes for the cool nights here?" Kirk twirled his finger around his cranium. "It's a mess in here."

"And yet you can't pick up the damned phone."

"I was trying to give you an out, woman. I wasn't just ignoring you."

"And now you're here to what? Ask me on a date?"

"No. I'm here to ask you out to eat."

She offered him a slow, furious blink. "So, a date?"

"I've come to the realization that I screwed up," Kirk said, sinking down onto the bed beside her. "I let us go too far physically before you saw what kind of man I am."

"And what kind of man are you?"

Honesty pooled in his dark eyes as he admitted, "The dangerous kind to give a tender heart to."

Oh, she understood. He was warning her off him.

"I don't want to go on a date with you if you're just going to push me away again. It makes all of this too hard."

"That's why I'm not calling it a date."

She wanted him. Not just physically, but she wanted to know everything about him. Wanted to possess him. Wanted to be the last set of lips he kissed for all his life. And yeah, she got how insane that was, but her heart had shackled itself to him, and she was in too deep to turn back from the potency of her feelings now. "Kirk, you feel big. I've been sleepwalking for so long, just trudging along with the world all blurred around me, out of control of my life and only living it halfway. But then you came along, and for the first time in as long as I can remember, everything seems so clear. And part of it is that I feel so damned relieved that I have the ability to *feel* after everything that happened. But if we aren't going anywhere, and if you're going to pull me in close only to shove me away again, over and over, that'll hurt me. And I think it'll hurt you, too. I don't want that. Go home, Kirk. Think about what you want from me, and next time you talk to me, be real clear because I suck at hints. If you don't feel like I'm big, too, then cut me loose."

Kirk scrubbed his hand down his dark, three-day stubble and stood. He paced back to her, adjusted his baseball cap over his head and left. The front door banging closed shook the bones of the house, and Alison closed her eyes against the pain in her chest. That was one of the hardest things she'd ever done, being that direct with a man she cared so deeply about, but he had to choose—in or out—because she wasn't going to be someone's *maybe*.

She needed more.

The front door creaked open and the loud, hollow sound of Kirk's boots echoed across the floor. His eyes were bright gold when he came to a stop in her doorway. "I'm not going to be any good at this."

She stood slowly. "I won't expect you to be any more than you are."

His chest heaved as he stared at her with those glowing eyes. So terrifying and beautiful all at once. Three more steps, and he pulled her to his chest hard. His heart pounded so fast against her cheek, and she closed her eyes, inhaling his scent. The smell of man and beast clashed. Body wash and fur. God, she loved this, being in his arms, feeling safe. She squeezed her eyes tighter. He wouldn't let her fall into the darkness. Not like the others. Kirk was too battle-hardened to go soft. He didn't see it, but she needed him just as he was. He was perfect, and he didn't even realize it.

"I want to take you out on a date." His voice was too low, too scratchy. "I'm already in this deeper than you can understand. It happens like that for shifters, and staying away from you is too damned hard. I'll take you on a date, and then another and another, until you are the one pushing me away."

"Why would I?"

"Because what can I give you, Ally? What could I possibly give to keep a woman like you happy? I work a labor job, and I'm content staying in one place. I can date you but, legally, that's where our relationship peaks. I live in a trailer park with a crew of fuck-ups. And I love them. I do. But you won't understand why we are the way we are."

"Maybe you should give me a chance to understand."

He inhaled deeply, then blew it out and buried his face against her neck. "You're terrifying."

She laughed because Kirk was admitting that she was scary? He, a freaking massive gorilla shifter with glowing eyes and a rumble in his throat, who could pull bullets from his arm without wincing. She was no threat to him. "No more running," she whispered.

"I won't." Kirk shook his head and eased back. He pulled off his baseball cap, turned it around, and put it on backward, then leaned down and kissed her. He was surprisingly gentle this time, hand on her neck, thumb stroking her cheek as he tilted her face back.

He brushed his tongue against the seam of her lips, asking to taste her, not demanding it like last time.

She smiled against his mouth and parted her lips for him. His kiss was slow and methodical. It was the knee-melting kind, where she felt like she was sinking closer to the floor and flying all at once. It was sparks on the edge of her vision and warming from the inside out. And right when she thought he would push for more, his erection thick and hard between them, he eased away and smiled at her like she was beautiful. "You should've let me run."

"Why is that?"

The humor dipped from his face, and his eyes were earnest when he murmured, "Because now you're mine."

# NINE

Alison had never lived in a small town before, but she had to admit, she liked how everyone seemed to know everyone. Even when she drove around, everyone on the road lifted two fingers off their steering wheels in a friendly wave. Out here, it was more wide open, not as cluttered like her life in Chicago had been. She'd lived and worked in the worst parts of town there, but here, she was awed by the scenery, the people, and even the cabin.

She'd never been much for nature because she hadn't been around it very much, but it was definitely growing on her. The clean air, the cordial atmosphere, the people...Kirk.

"Are you one of them vegetarians?" Kirk asked, his eyes narrowed into judgmental little slits.

"I eat everything. I just have one of those

fast metabolisms. Trust me, I don't look emaciated because I'm watching my figure." She swung her legs out of his car and slid her hand against his palm, allowing him to help her out. "I always wished I had curves like one of those pinup girls. You know, big boobs, hips for days, hourglass shape. It wasn't my dream to grow up to look like a green bean."

Kirk let off a booming, "Ha!" and shut her door behind her. "Woman, you don't look like any bean I've seen. Your figure is sexy as hell. Lithe and graceful like a cat. That's what I'm gonna call you. Ally Cat."

"I don't know if I like that. A street cat without a home?"

"Nah," Kirk said, turning on her. He squared up to her and pushed her short hair behind her ear. "You've been through it. A little banged up, but tough as all get-out. You know how to get things done because no one ever coddled you. Independent, headstrong badass, and if anyone wants to pet you, you'll make 'em earn it." He lowered his voice and said, "You'll make me earn it."

She searched his face to make sure he wasn't teasing, but he wasn't even smiling. No one had ever pegged her so accurately and in such a way that made her proud of who she was. In a soft voice, she admitted, "I like that name much better now."

"Moosey's has the best damned barbecue around, and I feel like my belly button is rubbing a burn on my backbone I'm so hungry."

"I could eat," she said coolly as he guided her around a giant rain puddle in the muddy parking lot.

He hesitated in front of a trio of open doors that seemed to be the entrance to a garage-themed restaurant. "Look, the food isn't the only reason I brought you here."

"Ulterior motives, huh? Spill it."

"You said earlier that I should give you a chance to meet my crew. Well, one of them works here. She's second in the Boarlander—"

"Audrey."

"Yeah." Kirk frowned. "I forget you probably have files on all of us."

Ally snorted. "Yeah, files I stopped reading. It didn't feel right reading someone else's intel on people who haven't done anything wrong. I wanted to form opinions of you guys on my own. Reading those files made me feel like I was stealing your stories. I would rather earn them."

Kirk drew back like she'd clawed him. "Really?"

"Yes, really. Is that her?" Alison waved to the leggy brunette wearing a pink Moosey's Bait and Barbecue shirt, cutoff jean shorts, and cowgirl boots. She wore a megawatt grin and was waving at them. Alison had seen Audrey's white tiger the first night she'd met the Boarlanders, but she'd never seen the woman half of her.

"Yeah, you need her," Kirk said in an odd voice.

"Need her how?" she asked as they made their way toward Audrey.

"To protect you from Clinton."

She opened her mouth to ask what the hell that meant, but Audrey hugged Kirk's shoulders and then arced her friendly smile to Alison.

"Oh, my God," she murmured, the grin falling from her lips. "You're the cop." Audrey took a step back and looked utterly confused. "I didn't recognize you out of uniform."

"Yeah," Alison said with a nervous laugh. "There aren't many parameters with my job out here. My boss said I was fine to wear the same clothes I did at my last position, and, well…I was undercover. I don't wear the uniform much."

Audrey flashed an intense look to Kirk, then back to Alison. "You gave Emerson the note. I know you didn't mean it for me, but you helped me to register with the Boarlanders before the deadline. So...thank you."

"I was really happy when I saw that you'd been able to do that. And I was cheering for Bash and Emerson, too. The law changes aren't my choice, nor do I agree with them. I'm just supposed to enforce them."

Audrey lifted her chin and stuck her hand out for a shake. "I'm Audrey."

Alison grinned and shook her hand. "I'm Ally."

Audrey pointed back and forth between Ally and Kirk. "And you two are here to conduct an interview? Oooor..."

"I'm taking her on a date," Kirk said, sliding his hand in soothing circles on Alison's back.

"Wait, wait, wait. You two are a thing?" Audrey yelled too loud.

"Audrey! Customers!" an older man called out. He wore a Moosey's shirt and stood behind a covered grill area outside.

"Sorry, Joey!" Audrey twitched her head toward the counter where, in fact, there was a couple staring up at the menu written on a huge wooden board over a meat cutting station. "Walk with me." In a whisper-scream, she said, "You two are a thing? Does Harrison know? Or Damon? Or Clinton? Does anyone know?"

"You do. And I'm pretty sure Damon figured it out. And Mason," Kirk admitted, casting Alison a quick glance. "He's been my sounding board."

"You mean he was who you talked to when you were avoiding the hell out of me," Alison muttered.

"Oh, he avoided you?" Audrey giggled. "That doesn't work. When a shifter animal chooses a mate, it's done."

"Wait, what?" Alison asked.

Kirk pursed his lips and shook his head at Audrey like she was crazy.

"What do you mean when an animal chooses a mate?" she pushed. They were not done with that little bomb Audrey had just dropped.

A sharp rumble came from Kirk's chest, and the air felt muggier, which made no sense because they'd just come under the protection of the barbecue joint and there were fans up in the top corners of the room.

Audrey's face had gone comically blank. Urgently, Alison said, "Tell me!"

"Great dusty balls, I ain't good at lyin', Kirk," Audrey muttered. "You should've told her."

"Dammit, Audrey. She isn't a shifter like you. She's human. Different timeline." Oh, now Kirk looked pissed.

Audrey jacked up her dark eyebrows and looked stubborn. "Emerson is human, and her and Bash's timeline was just as short as me and Harrison's. Maybe shorter!"

"Nye!" Kirk said, slashing his hand through the air.

Audrey's mouth flopped open, and she looked like one of those cartoon characters with smoke blowing out of their ears. With fire in her brown eyes, she rounded on Alison and whispered, "His gorilla picked you. I can tell. You're it for him, and if you stick around, he'll be an awesome mate for you. He won't be able to help himself. Your happiness will be all he'll think about."

Kirk wrapped his hands around air in a choking motion. Audrey flipped him off before she turned and made her way behind the counter.

Alison was dumbfounded. Shocked was

too small a word. His mate? Mate? That sounded huge. How did she not know the exact meaning of this? She was a police officer. She should've been prepped better than this. She should've known the culture of the people she was watching, protecting, and conversing with. But with Audrey's declaration, she now felt in way over her head.

Kirk felt big, and now he would never be able to deny it. She was big, too.

"Your animal picked me?" she asked in a strange, husky voice she barely recognized.

"I was thinking we should split some jalapeño sausage."

"Kirk."

"You're right. Ribs are better."

"Kirk."

"Cheesy corn is a must."

"Kirk! Am I your mate?"

"I don't want to talk about this here."

Alison gritted her teeth and squeezed his hands, leveled him with a fierce look. "Tell me quick, Kirk."

"Yes." His voice cracked on the harsh word, and now he wouldn't meet her gaze. Jerkily, he nodded his chin. "I chose you. I didn't mean for it to happen. Didn't want it."

That stung like a slap on cold skin. "Why?"

"Because you can do better."

"That right there is a bullcrap cop-out. Why didn't you tell me?"

Kirk crossed his arms over his muscular, barrel chest and sighed. "Because now you'll be the one running."

# TEN

"Okay." In her lap, Alison readjusted the to-go boxes of food they hadn't eaten. "Okay," she repeated for the tenth time since she'd found out she was someone's...mate. That word felt huge.

"You're freaking out." Kirk said low. Even though he was the epitome of relaxed, leaned back against the seat of his Mustang, arm draped over the steering wheel as they coasted up the winding mountain road, his eyes had been that eerie yellow color that said his animal was just under the surface.

Posturing seemed to be a big thing for Kirk, but maybe that was important to all gorilla shifters. Or all shifters. Crap on a cracker, she regretted not doing more research. She was a friggin' cop after all, and she'd just adopted this if-it's-important-they'll-tell-me attitude. That wasn't her. She'd never been a go-with-the-flow type of girl. She'd always been a know-as-much-as-possible-so-she-could-freaking-survive type of person.

"I haven't been upfront with you," she murmured, holding onto the handle on the door as Kirk sped around a curve in the road. "There is a reason I was picked for this task force. Or not task force as much as a post up here in the mountains."

Kirk tossed her a dangerous glance. "Are you spying on us?"

Anger blasted through her veins that he still thought she was some kind of snitch on him and his people. She took an extra beat to steady her temper before she responded. "No, I'm not a spy. But I think you should know the whole story before you pick me."

"Too damned late, Holman. It happened that first night I saw you in the woods. Sleeping with me only made it ironclad. You still have an out. You do. I'm not pressuring you to continue with me, wouldn't want to force a pairing with anyone. I don't want to drag you along beside me for this."

"Do you have an out?"

Kirk clenched his teeth so hard a muscle

twitched in his jaw. "Too late for me. Like Audrey said, you're it."

"It's a lot for a first date."

"And you're flighty, which is why I have been trying to keep this slow and casual."

"But I shot you!"

"And I still couldn't bring myself to be mad at you!"

"I was pulled from active duty," she blurted out.

Kirk's angry expression faltered. "What?"

"You should know what kind of terrible person you got mixed up with, Kirk. You should know just in case your animal can take that decision back. In case you want to pick someone else." She sucked in a shaking breath and explained, "I was working undercover at a cocaine factory. It was this huge setup, and they had a guy who had been undercover for years and worked his way up the chain of command. But they needed someone who was always there, taking note of who was involved, who they dealt with, how much product was moved. Someone who could get their hands on documents and proof when the time came."

"You?"

"Yeah. I was young and looked hard. I was a street rat and knew the language, knew how to play the part. I landed a job cutting coke from bricks and bagging it up to deal. I was lucky. That's what my handlers said, but they weren't there. They didn't understand the cost, or maybe they didn't care. I lived in a roach-infested one-room apartment at night, and during the day, I worked in a dark, dank, hot room. And I wasn't allowed to wear clothes."

Kirk swallowed hard and looked sick. Slowly, he pulled over to the side of the road and put the car into park. "Why not?"

"Lots of reasons. Fabric is flammable, less risk of us stealing product if we were naked, the powder could've got on our clothes and tipped off drug dogs. Lots of reasons were given, but it didn't take away from the fact that I was nothing. Naked. Invisible if I was lucky. The tattoos were a way of feeling covered. I started getting ink the second week I worked there."

"Because you didn't like people looking at you?"

"One in particular. Riggs was the undercover cop who had risen mid-level in the operation. I respected him. I was uncomfortable being naked in front of him because…" Her cheeks burned, and she dipped her gaze to her clasped hands on top of the to-go boxes. "I cared for him. He openly flirted with me in the factory. It was expected, and lots of the guards did it. One of the lower-level guards had taken a fancy to me, and his attention was terrifying, but Riggs swooped in there and took me under his wing. Told the guy if he ever even looked at me sideways, he would rip his throat out. And he played his part well. Too well maybe. I don't know. I grew feelings. I looked forward to seeing him on the days he was supposed to come in. I felt safe when he came in, but how seriously could he take me if I was naked? If I was always cowed, just observing the operation, cutting coke, day after day, doing my part. Doing a job that kept me less than. We went on like that for two years and, eventually, it didn't feel like undercover work anymore. I gave into the show. It felt like my life."

"Where is Riggs now?"

She swallowed bile and squeezed her eyes tightly closed at the memory of him lying on the floor, gasping for breath, eyes on her, silently telling her not to give herself away. "They made him as a cop, and they killed him. They made an example of him in front of all of us. It was slow." A tear slid down the bridge of her nose, and she shook her head, desperate to ease the pain in her chest. "I wanted to stop after he died. Wanted to grieve and run far away from that hell hole, quit my job, the whole nine yards. But I was cracking that operation wide open with my intel, and we still needed to connect big names to it. I was supposed to just carry on, but I couldn't get Riggs out of my head. The guilt... I didn't do anything."

"You couldn't have. They would've killed you, too."

"I know, but most days, I thought maybe that would have been better. Easier."

"Fuck," Kirk gritted out, wrapping his hand around hers.

"He was the only friend I made in all that time. The only one I allowed myself to have. And when he was gone, the man who killed him started looking at me with this sick hunger in his eyes. So, one day, he took me into one of the back rooms, and I'd been prepped, you know? I was supposed to do whatever I had to do not to get made, but he'd killed Riggs, and I couldn't just spread my legs for him. Couldn't." She wiped her tears from her face with the sleeve of her shirt and looked up at Kirk so he could see what a monster she was when she whispered, "And so I killed him."

Kirk pulled her in tight against his chest. His arms shook around her, his heartbeat pounding too fast. He should know about the dark parts of her before he picked her, though.

"I barely made it out of there, and after that, I couldn't go back. I'd compromised all those years of work. I'd failed Riggs. Failed my department. Failed myself. My intel gave the proof to put a lot of the low-level players away, but we didn't get the big fish because I cracked. I failed my psych evals with flying colors. PTSD was the diagnosis that got my ass dumped onto deskwork, and eventually they got tired of denying my requests for anything else to do, so they sent me here. I'm not here to spy on you, Kirk. This job is my punishment."

"Why, Ally? Why would you sign up for something like that?"

"Because what choice did I have? I remember my mom. She was beautiful and funny when I was a little kid, but then there were the years of addiction. Of her being on the streets and not at home with me. Of her being strung out, slurring her words, bringing all these guys by, and not caring for me. She had no idea who my dad was, so she had no financial help there. I was taken away from her, and I didn't know how to feel. Relieved that I would have somewhere safe to sleep? Angry that she didn't try harder? Sad that I wasn't enough to keep her straight? She got locked up and the state kept me, and all the sudden, the only person I recognized in my life was one of my mom's friends, Regina. She visited and gave me letters my mom mailed me from prison. She even tried to adopt me, but she had a criminal record, and it never went through. No one wanted an angry ten year old. People want cute babies to raise, so I aged out of the girls' home. Do you know what percent of kids go homeless who age out? Go to the streets? Get addicted? It's a ridiculous number, and I didn't want to be another statistic. I wanted to do something that could help people. And I know that sounds fucked up to you, because who was I possibly helping by sitting in that damned drug house bagging up coke? But I was taking major operations off the streets that had ruined my mom. I was the good guy." She was crying now, punching her words out through her sobs. She hadn't talked about this with anyone other than her required therapist in Chicago, but this time felt different. She wasn't having to watch her answers or keep details hidden. She could unload to Kirk because he made her feel safe and he wasn't going to take her job away if she didn't give a good enough answer. With every gritty thing she exposed about herself, Kirk hugged her tighter.

"I didn't have opportunities coming at me from all sides. I had one offer to train for a real, paying job, and I could hold onto it and own it, or I could be just like the other kids who aged out and hit the ground too hard to ever recover. I just thought you should know all of it before you called me your mate."

"You're not scared of that word," he murmured, more stunned statement than question.

Alison sniffed, then laughed. "No. It felt damn good to hear someone pick me. Not because of what I look like or what I could do for them, but just because I'm *it* for someone. And not just any someone, but *you*. You feel like mine too, Kirk. And I know how fucked up that sounds because of the human timeline and all, but every instinct I have screams that you are this safe house for me. Like you could be happiness. Like my road has forked—one path leads off into these haunted woods, one leads off a cliff, and the middle one is you. Hands in your pockets, smile on your face, Boarlander woods behind you, just waiting for me to stop considering the self-destructive paths and choose you back."

"And do you?" Kirk asked low, like the answer meant something. Like it meant everything.

"Are you sure you still want me after everything I've told you?"

Kirk unbuckled her seat belt, slid his seat back, and pulled her onto his lap like she weighed nothing. Burying his face against her neck, he inhaled deeply, then murmured, "Nothing you just told me scares me off, Ally Cat. It only makes me like you more."

Her face caved, and more tears stained his shirt. What a beautiful thing to hear after everything she'd been through. After all the damage, she was still enough for Kirk. Clutching his shirt and hugging him tight, she whispered, "Then yes. I choose you, too."

# ELEVEN

Alison tried not to roll her eyes as the early twenty-something shifter groupies packed in an old Volkswagen van begged for her to let them pass.

Too bad for them, she and Finn had built the road blocks yesterday to keep the boldest of the groupies abiding by the rules.

"Sorry ladies. There is nothing up there for you."

"False," the blond with the movie star glasses sneered from behind the wheel. "Bangaboarlander dot com just added three new shifters a couple days ago."

Alison frowned. "What are you talking about?"

"The shifter matchmaking website? Three new males were announced to be looking for mates. Three shifters..." She pointed to her and her two friends. "Three mates."

"I call Kirk," a buxom brunette said excitedly.

"No one calls Kirk," Alison gritted out.

"Yes, I just did. He looks hot as fuck in his picture. Look." The brunette handed her phone out the driver's side window, and Alison squinted at the small, glowing screen.

In his picture, Kirk was looking off to the side, muscular, thick neck flexed, aviator sunglasses blocking his eyes from the sun, lips curled up in a naughty, sexpot smile, with a white V-neck T-shirt under an unbuttoned blue flannel shirt, his muscular arms straining against the thin material. His hair looked windblown and sexy, and if her ovaries were currently doing a fireworks show in her middle, it was no wonder why brunette was calling dibs.

*Kirk Slater, 6'3", quiet, loves to hug, is a demon in the sack, and ready for an immediate mate, great second best friend. If you want this man and to birth all his gorilla shifter babies, contact him here.*

There was an arrow pointing to a *Poke Me Hard* button, and underneath was a gif of a shirtless Kirk striding by in slow motion, running his hand through his wet hair and giving a panty-melting smile. It played on an ovary-exploding loop of hotness.

"Oh, my damn," she murmured. This was not okay, and now her insides had turned green. "How many people can see this?"

Brunette leaned over her friend's lap and pointed. "His page has gotten over seven thousand hits since it went live a couple days ago. But realistically, probably a hundred of those visits are me. I can't stop watching the gif!"

This is what rage felt like. Molten lava in her middle, tingling fingers, an all-consuming urge to break things. Carefully, Alison handed the phone back and ground out, "I'm sorry you traveled here all the way from..."

"South Dakota," Blondie offered helpfully.

"Yes, South Dakota, but you can't just show up to their houses. Try the contact button, or better yet, attend a Shifter Night in Saratoga. They'll come down to mingle if they're really looking for mates. Now go on. You've been waiting here for an hour, and I'm about to start handing out tickets." For what, she hadn't a clue, but the bluff worked because the trio of beauties pulled out from in front of her cabin, their botoxed lips in a pout.

Finn was chewing a long cord of rope

candy, an annoying smile on his face. "They were hot."

"But mostly obnoxious." Alison made her way into her cabin and stripped out of her uniform.

"You look mad," Finn said from right behind her, smacking loudly.

"Do you mind?" she yelled, shoving her legs into her jean shorts.

"Not at all."

Idiot. She'd had her suspicions she wasn't the only one being punished with this job, and apparently she'd been right. When she'd searched for dirt on Finn, a rap sheet had come up of sexual harassment warnings filed by other female cops in his precinct. He'd been given a leave of absence and somehow ended up here, with her. Goodie.

She shoved him out of her bedroom doorway and slammed the door, then pulled on a tank top, red to represent her rage. Kirk was gonna get it. And by it, she meant the verbal mauling of a lifetime. Bangaboarlander.com? What the hell? No one was supposed to be banging Kirk but her!

"Mind the office," she demanded as she grabbed a hoodie and stomped across the small porch.

Bangaboarlander. Mother fluffer. What was she to him? His Monday mate? He still needed to fill the rest of the days of the week? She was going to kill him, then revive him, then kill him again. She hopped into the SUV she'd been issued and pulled out of the yard. When she looked back in the rearview mirror, Finn was glaring suspiciously at her, arms crossed over his chest, stick of rope candy hanging from his hand like a ready sword.

But right about now, she gave exactly zero fucks about his opinion. Why? Because he was a lady groper, and he had no place being judgmental of her life choices.

She pulled around the road block, mud shooting up around her like a rooster tail, then skidded and straightened out onto the road. Two days ago. He'd uploaded his profile two days ago, so after his gorilla had "chosen" her, after they'd slept together, and after her whole heart had latched onto him. She hated games. Hated. Them.

She nearly went up on two wheels turning right onto the gravel road that would lead her to Boarland Mobile Park. She'd never been jealous in her life, but this was different. She'd bared her soul to a man who was playing her. He'd sympathized with her admission of what had happened to Riggs, and all the while, he was online looking for groupie pussy? Everything was bathed in shades of red.

She came to a skidding stop under the Boarland Mobile Park sign and leaned forward over her steering wheel. She blinked hard and shook her head to clear the hallucination she was clearly having.

A dark-headed giant of a muscle man sat in a plastic lawn chair held together with strips of duct tape. In his hands was a fishing pole, and the end of the line disappeared into a giant pothole in the middle of the road.

Alison's windshield wipers dragged loudly over the sparse raindrops on her window. Sebastian Kane was fully bearded, wearing a damp white T-shirt and holey jeans, looking completely relaxed as he fished out of the pothole. Beside him, his mate and wife, Emerson Kane, was draped across another plastic chair, white sunglasses on, her curly black hair gathered at the top of her head in a wild bun, and was reading a book under a bright pink umbrella. She and Bash would be the vision of contentment if it weren't for the giant fire blazing in the middle of the street behind them. And several yards from the fire, a sandy blond-haired man in yellow eighties-style short shorts and matching tube socks lay shirtless on the ground, hugging a half empty bottle of cheap whiskey.

In a daze, Alison cut the engine, shoved her door open and slid out, her anger evaporating by the second.

Bash pointed with his index finger and grinned. "Police woman. I like your tattoos, and your face is red, my second favorite color."

Emerson shoved her sunglasses over her hair. "Are you here for a meeting with Harrison or something?"

"Uh, no. I'm here to see Kirk."

"Kirk!" Bash yelled.

The man on the ground didn't even flinch. She was growing more and more concerned at his proximity to the fire. "Is he dead or just sleeping?"

"Who, Clinton?" Emerson asked, glancing at the man in the road. "Nah. Bash told Clinton the potholes in the trailer park needed to be fixed."

"And Clinton being the poop chute he is said the road is fine as it is. Which clearly," Bash said, looking around at the destroyed road, "it ain't."

"So then Bash said the potholes were so big he could catch a fish in one," Emerson said.

Bash moved a toothpick from one corner of his mouth to the other side. "And then Clinton said if I caught a fish in one, we could fix the road, and he wouldn't throw a piss-fit." Bash pulled the line of his fishing pole from the deep pothole, and Alison yelped as he pulled out a sizeable flopping fish.

"Oh, my gosh, you actually caught a fish in there?"

Emerson wrapped her arms around her stomach and giggled. "No. Bash caught the fish in the river and brought it back here. When Clinton saw it, he went into a rage and set Ant-hillia on fire."

"Ant-hillia?" Alison asked.

"Yeah, that's the giant anthill that Clinton has been waging war on. He keeps kicking it down, but the ants keep building it back up."

"Why doesn't he poison them?"

"Because he said there's no honor in poison," Bash said with a matter-of-fact nod of his head.

"So he set fire to it?"

"Yep," Bash said. "Doused it in gasoline and lit it up because he was so pissed at losing the bet. And then instead of bleeding me like he usually does, he drank himself stupid and passed out in the street."

Emerson grinned. "Progress."

Alison's head was beginning to hurt.

Harrison, the titan, musclebound behemoth alpha of the Boarlanders, kicked open the door of the first trailer on the right, gave her a suspicious glare, then walked past them all with a sloshing bucket in his hand.

When he dumped it over Clinton, the man sat up and gasped out, "Nipples."

"Your pants are about to light on fire," Harrison gritted out.

"So you dumped the water on me?" Clinton slurred through a deep frown. "Why didn't you put out the fire?"

"You started the fire. You put it out!"

"Nipples is the name of a mouse," Bash explained through a distracted smile as he settled the fish back in the pothole pond. "Clinton is mad because we wouldn't let him have one of her babies for his trailer. Everyone got one but Harrison, who said he didn't want mouse shit in his food, and Clinton because he can barely take care of himself."

"Shut up, Bash!" Clinton said, struggling to his feet.

Kirk came out of the first trailer on the left with an armload of what looked like ceiling tiles. "Hey," he said, coming to a stop on his porch. He tossed the demolition materials over the side of the railing into a knee-high pile of debris and pulled his gloves off as he jogged down his porch stairs. He yanked out a pair of earbuds blaring music, and his face transformed into a big grin. Kirk cupped his hand at his mouth and yelled, "Hey, Clinton!"

"What?" the swaying man demanded in a grumpy tone.

"One, your shorts are too short and your dick is hanging out, and two, I'd like you to meet my mate."

"I don't even care anymore," Clinton said.

Bash and Emerson snickered quietly.

"You don't care about me bringing a girl into the trailer park?" Kirk asked.

"We're already going to hell, Kirk," Clinton slurred. "Might as well do it thoroughly." He stumbled off toward a trailer at the back of the park, mumbling to himself. Alison couldn't understand a word he said until he yelled over his shoulder, "Maybe I'll get a million mates!"

"I like when Clinton is drunk," Bash said in a giddy voice.

Kirk came at her with his arms out like he was going in for a hug, but her anger was back now, and she slapped his pec before he could embrace her. It stung her palm, but he didn't even flinch. Now she was even madder.

"What's wrong?" he asked, his dark brows lowering with concern.

"Am I your mate, Kirk? *Am I*?"

Kirk narrowed his eyes into wary little slits. "Yeees."

"Then why did you just upload your profile to diddleaboarlander dot com two days ago?" Yep, she was shouting, but so what?

"Bangaboarlander dot com?" Emerson asked.

"I didn't," Kirk barked out. "I've never even been on that damned site. You want to blame someone for uploading anything about me, blame Willa."

"Of the Gray Backs? Why the hell would she upload anything about you? Kirk Slater, six foot three, loves hugging, ready for a mate." Or something like that. "Sound familiar? Seven thousand hits from horny women!"

"Uh, that wasn't Willa," Bash said.

"Damn straight. It was this two-timing, conniving, pussy-chasing liar!" Alison bent down and picked up a handful of mud, then chucked it at Kirk. It splatted satisfyingly across his neck and cheek.

He jerked in surprise and closed his eyes. And when he opened them again, they were glowing a flaming gold.

"I posted that," Bash called. "I did them for Clinton and Mason, too, because I want them to be happy like me."

"W-what?" Alison asked, wiping her muddy hand on her shorts.

"I like the way you cuss," Bash said, his smile growing uncertain. "And you throw good."

Kirk wiped a glob of brown goop from his face and gritted out, "Bash, could you kindly take that profile down? Because apparently, I'm mated to a *crazy woman*." He spun and strode with purpose toward his trailer.

"Ooooh, Kirk, I'm so sorry," she said, jogging after him. "It's nice to meet all of you!" she called over her shoulder, waving with her mud-smeared hand.

Harrison stood by the simmering fire in the middle of the road with his hands on his hips, glaring at her, while Emerson grinned from ear-to-ear. "Welcome to the trailer park!"

"Nice to meet you without a gun in your hand," Bash called just before she followed Kirk into his trailer.

"I swear I'm not crazy. I just, whoa, what happened to this place?" She stood in what looked like a living room, if said room had actual walls and a ceiling. Wires were exposed everywhere, and she could see the innards of the trailer on display. No insulation.

Kirk paced a small dining area, hands on his hips, and a terrifying sound rattled from his throat. He jammed his finger at a sizeable puddle of water on the floor. "Leaky roof, waterlogged ceiling, the insulation in the walls has disintegrated to nothing, and I have to rewire this place so it doesn't burn to the ground." His eyes sparked as he glared at her.

"I'm really sorry I jumped to conclusions."

"You know what I'm doing this all for?" he asked, spreading his arms out.

Alison scrunched up her nose. "Me?"

"Yeah, you. Logging season is almost through, and I'm not a Boarlander. Not officially. I'm supposed to go back to the Lowlanders, but that means leaving here. Leaving you. Fixing up this place is me toying with the idea that I can have you."

"It's a nice trailer," she said, trying to hide a grin. "Any woman would be lucky to shack up with you here."

"Okay," he said, rolling his eyes. "Enough. I know this old singlewide isn't a big deal to you, and yeah, I know this place isn't exactly a castle, but I thought if I fixed it up, I would have a better chance of tempting you to stay."

"Where else would I go?"

"Ally, you and I both know your job here isn't permanent. And I can't give you my last name or a claiming mark. Not anymore. So this is what I have—a refurbished, thirty-year-old singlewide and a crew of dipshits. Contain your excitement."

"Well, I just turned away a van-load of pretty girls who would sell their fingers to have a shot at hooking up with you, so maybe you have more to offer than you thought."

"Oh, yeah?" His eyebrows lifted, and humor danced in his darkening eyes. "Like what?"

"Like that sex-mobile you drive around." She approached slowly and murmured, "Vroom, vroom." Alison wrapped her arms around his waist and rested her chin on his chest, looking up at him with an apologetic grin. "And in the words of one of your groupies, 'you're sexy as fuck,' and though she was probably dumb as a brick, I happen to agree with her. I'm going to need a copy of the gif Bash used on your profile for my lady spank bank."

"What gif?" he asked, looking troubled.

"No shirt, slow motion smile as you strode

by. It was hot."

"Oh, geez. Bash probably took that while we were swimming at Bear Trap Falls the other day. He means well but, damn, he meddles."

"It's a horrible invasion of privacy and also a form of identity theft, but under all that, it's kind of sweet. He wants you to be happy."

"It's true!" Bash yelled from outside the trailer. "I do want you to be happy!"

"Bash, we need space to talk," Kirk called out.

"But I can hear you from inside my house. What's a lady spank bank?"

Oh, well that was just great. Shifter hearing was much better than she'd realized. That or the gutted walls in Kirk's trailer were giving zero sound barrier.

Kirk twitched his head toward the back door and pulled her hand until they were outside. She was apparently hiking too slowly through the piney woods behind his house because he bent at the knees and gave her a piggy-back ride through the ferns and brush.

After a few minutes of nothing but the sound of the birds in the canopy, Kirk said, "It really bothers me that you didn't trust me."

"It wasn't that I didn't trust you, Kirk. It

was scary hearing you tell me about the family group you grew up with, how there was one dominant male and a bunch of females, and now your people are having to figure out whether to pick one mate or stick to family groups. And I researched it, the dynamics of the family and all that. Maybe female gorilla shifters are okay sharing a mate, but I'm not."

"Okay," he said, sounding troubled. Kirk set her down and ran his hands through his hair, then nodded and repeated, "Okay. That's fair, and it makes sense, but like I told you before, I'm not one of the family group males. Not anymore, and maybe I never really was. I didn't like that my mom only got a fraction of my dad's attention. I didn't like watching her light up when he paid her a compliment, but delve into depression when he was giving other females more attention. She lived and breathed for time with him. Growing up knowing that I was going to have to manage time between a lot of females was completely overwhelming. I didn't like it, but that's all I knew. And most of the time, the females seemed to genuinely care about the male that took care of them. So as I got older, I came around to the idea. I decided I would do it better. Have less females, care for them better, protect them better. But then this dominant female rose in power, and she changed everything for the worse. Fiona started pulling females from groups and moving them around, giving them to males they hadn't chosen for genetic advantages. She wanted to make stronger gorilla shifter children because she was convinced our people had gone soft. And eventually, she began choosing the females for each male. She created these huge groups under one male, and the other males were given guard duties. They were in charge of making sure the silverbacks she chose to father the next generation were kept out of trouble, and were kept clean and pure."

"You were a guard?"

Kirk nodded once. "I was dominant, bigger than all my half-brothers, and had come to an age where my animal instincts called for a family. A female and babies to protect. It's all I could think about. All I wanted. Fuck." Kirk clenched his jaw and shot a hard look up through the branches of the trees. "Let's walk, or I won't be able to do this."

Silently, Alison kept pace beside him. She knew she shouldn't touch him right now because Kirk's voice had gone deep and feral and his entire body rigid. His eyes were glowing that sunny gold, and he made the air feel like it had weight, but she couldn't *not* touch him when he was letting her in. Hesitating only a moment, she slipped her hand into his and bumped his shoulder.

Kirk gave her a slight smile, but it didn't reach his eyes. "Fiona chose me for guard duty, along with this asshole named Rhett, and she assigned us to her prize silverback, Kong."

"King Kong," she said softly as it clicked. "Of the Lowlanders."

"Yeah, and he's a brawler. He's the first silverback I ever met who felt more dominant than me. And so I did the job Fiona assigned me. And I watched him fall for a girl in town. Layla. He tried to keep her at a distance. She was feeling something for him, too. I never believed in fate or anything like that, but those two were on this collision course, and I couldn't stop it. After a while, I didn't even want to. I wanted Kong to be happy, and he wanted a single mate and children he could raise himself because, deep down, that's what I wanted, too. And the more I covered for him with Rhett, the more I let him slip into this relationship with a human, the more I knew Fiona would kill me for failing her." Kirk shrugged, then pulled Alison against his side,

124

draped his heavy arm around her shoulders. "I felt empty. Kong's gorilla stifled my instincts to want anything for myself. My whole life was devoted to keeping someone I respected unhappy. Fiona was going to off me. Everything had gone sideways, and there was no way out of it."

"So what did you do?"

"I made a stand with Kong. I didn't have anything to live for, but I liked Layla, and I wanted Kong happy. Our people were so fucked up, but he had this chance to be okay with his mate, and I was grasping onto anything that gave me purpose." Kirk kissed her hairline. "We'd chosen right when we moved here. We found unexpected allies. Kong killed Rhett, and when Fiona and all her guards came for her prize male, Kong and I didn't face her alone. The Gray Backs went to battle for him too, and that dragon the humans are so afraid of ended Fiona and her reign. She'd been building an unwilling army with the silverbacks she wouldn't allow to breed, but Damon freed us. Freed me."

"But...you pledged as a Lowlander. You still pledged with your people."

"With Kong. He's a good man, and he and Layla are trying for a baby. And Kong's mom,

Josephine, is in the group. It might not be the life I wanted, but I got to be around good people. It was okay for a while. I was almost happy. I worked at Kong's sawmill and even stayed in a spare room of his and Layla's, but it was like watching the life I wanted through a window. Only I didn't have the drive to actively find a mate because Kong's animal keeps mine in check. I don't think he even meant to. I started breathing easier when he released me to come up here and help out the Boarlanders for a logging season."

"That's the decision Damon was talking about," she murmured as it all clicked into place. "You are struggling with the decision of whether to move back to Saratoga and rejoin the Lowlanders."

Kirk huffed a breath and pulled her to a stop at the edge of a sandy beach on a river bank. To the right, there was a path up a cliff and a gorgeous waterfall tumbling over the edge. This was where she'd seen him and the Boarlanders for the first time when she'd come to retrieve Emerson.

"He's been calling me."

"Who?"

"Kong. I've been avoiding the talk. I know he wants me to come back to the sawmill. To his family group, but I don't know what to say. Not yet."

"What do you want to do? What do you imagine your future like, Kirk?"

She could see the moment he shut down. It was there in his eyes. The spark of conversation was snuffed out as the instant his face closed off. She hated that—his ability to push and pull so easily. Instead of answering her, Kirk pulled off his shirt and kicked out of his work boots.

She watched sadly as he shucked his clothes completely and strode into the waves, then disappeared under the dark water, aimed for the waterfall. And as he cut gracefully through the waves, it struck her for the first time that she loved him.

She'd never loved anyone. She hadn't allowed herself to, but Kirk—hot and cold, sweet and hard, strong, protective, scared-of-affection Kirk—had drawn it from her. He hadn't asked for her heart. He'd simply plucked it from her chest and held it gently, then dared her to come take it back from him. She didn't even want to because at least she was capable of deep emotion. Of deep adoration. Of deep love.

It had taken someone who was damaged

like her to give her this completely normal moment. This insecure, breathless, hope-filled, human moment that took a shifter to create.

Alison peeled out of her clothes. She was ready for him to see all of her. He'd tried to share all of himself, but he wasn't strong enough yet, and that was okay. She would be patient. But she was already there—ready for *all-in*.

Alison stepped into the waves and stood on the sandy bottom for a moment, water lapping at her bare thighs as she took in the roiling dark clouds over the mountains. In the distance, lightning flashed through the sky in blinding veins of electricity. The storm would be here in half an hour, she guessed.

She held her breath and dove into the water, then swam toward the falls as long as her lungs could stand it. When she broke the surface, she was right by the pounding water. She inhaled deeply and ducked under. It was beautiful beneath the surface. Muted rays of light illuminated the underwater world, and bubbles danced toward the surface. Alison swam deep enough to avoid the harsh falling water on her back, then came up for air on the other side. Kirk sat on a ledge just under the water's surface, chest heaving as he stared at the underside of the waterfall.

With a slow blink, he lowered his lightened gold eyes to hers. "I see you."

With a frown, she cut through the water to where he sat. She rested between his legs, kicking at the waves languidly. "What do you mean?"

"You asked me how I imagine my future, and I see you."

"That scares you."

Kirk ducked his chin to his chest and snorted. "Nothing scared me before you came along, and suddenly I have this huge thing to protect."

"You don't have to protect me."

"No, I mean, I have a shot at happiness, and it's terrifying to think it's up to me to keep it intact. I have this beautiful woman, and all my life I've screwed up. Couldn't keep things together. Couldn't do what I was supposed to. And I can't bind you to me, Ally. I can't put my last name on you or claim you. I'll just have to stomach this feeling that you'll really see me and leave when I disappoint you."

"You silly man," she murmured, pressing her breasts against the rock he sat on so she could be closer to him. "You're the only one who has ever fit me. Where am I gonna go?

This place," she said, rolling her gaze over the rocky cliff face behind him, "feels more like home to me than any other."

"How?"

"Because you're here. And that bullshit about me not having your last name or not claiming me..." She pressed her finger against the bullet hole scar on his shoulder. "You already bear my mark."

With a slight frown, Kirk looked at his shoulder. "You shot me. That's not a claiming mark."

"Says who? I gave it to you. I've told you you're mine. I've chosen you. I marked you, and I'm not going anywhere. Rules be damned, we're bound. Now, ask me what I see in my future!"

Kirk traced the intricate tattoos along her collar bone and whispered, "How do you imagine your future?"

She smiled up at him. "I see you, too."

"You do?" He said it with his head cocked like he didn't believe her.

She laughed. For an intelligent man, he could be dense when it came to matters of the heart. "Obviously, Kirk. I came up here ready to roll some heads because I thought you were looking for another mate. I felt like a jealous psychopath."

"Yeah, that was crazy," he muttered through a baiting grin. "I have to admit, though, I liked seeing you all riled up over me." He pushed her damp hair from her forehead and murmured, "Possessive little Ally Cat."

She clamped her teeth onto his rib cage and grinned. "Mine, mine, mine. Now stop pushing me away. I don't like chasing you."

"Do that again," he whispered, his eyes sparking with desire.

Her heart banged against her chest at how hungry he looked. Slowly, deliberately, she bit the skin over his ribs again, harder this time. Kirk groaned and rocked his body toward her as if he couldn't help himself. She'd left a circle of indentations where her teeth had almost broken his skin, and suddenly, she couldn't remember exactly what the new law stated. Did it include humans biting shifters? She thought not. And even if so, she was having a really hard time caring right now. Those law changes were fucked up anyway. She knew the people here better now. Kirk wasn't just trying to procreate. None of them were. They were just looking for ways to feel like they belonged to the people they loved. And she loved him. Loved him.

Her breath hitched as she climbed onto his lap, and she gasped at how hard his erection was as she straddled him. The waves lapped at her ribs. She gripped the back of his hair with one hand, then ran her fingernails lightly down the scar on his shoulder—the one she'd given him. It was unfinished. His admission that it wasn't a claiming mark said as much.

Alison rocked her hips forward, stroking her sex against his hard cock. Kirk gripped her waist and pulled her closer. She sipped at his lips, bit his bottom lip, then moved to his neck, where she teased him there with her teeth, too. This was his warning, and if he didn't want this, she would stop the instant he told her to. But Kirk bucked against her, and as if he could read her mind, guided her head down his neck toward his bullet scar.

His muscles were taut, bulging, flexed just under the mark, like he was ready. Prepared. Wanting. "Do it," he whispered, brushing his hand up her spine, then gripping the back of her neck.

*Don't think.*

Alison bit him. Hard. Harder.

"More," he gritted out. "Make it count."

She tasted iron but still she clamped down until her jaw wouldn't tighten any further.

This moment was huge. It was sluffing off any remaining fear and diving in, heart first. There was no taking back her feelings after this. No taking back how devoted she already was. She pulled away and stared at the mark she'd made. A perfect circle around the bullet hole. It looked like an eclipse.

But her face fell, along with her heart, because it still didn't feel finished. Stupid law. It wasn't right. Wasn't fair.

"You aren't like the bear shifters. Your bite won't Turn me," she whispered, trying to understand why anyone would take this away from Kirk. From his people.

"No," he said, his Adam's apple dipping into his muscular throat with his hard swallow.

Not fair. Not right.

His gaze dipped to the mark she'd made, then to her tattoos. He traced the script in her half-sleeve of ink. *Remember.* Her reminder to never give into the darkness like Mom had. Eventually, she would tell him the story of every one of the tattoos, because he deserved to know all of her. That was the biggest gift she had to offer, and no one had come close to it before.

Kirk blinked slowly, then lifted an

inhuman gold gaze to hers. "Turn around," he murmured.

The sound of his deep timbre brushed up her spine and gave her a delicious shiver. Slowly, she gave him her back, arching it so she could feel his erection against her sex. Resting her hands on his knees, she looked back over her shoulder so she could watch his face when he saw all of her ink for the first time.

He dragged that sexy gaze down every inch of her tattooed back, then lifted her by the waist to take in the rest that curved around her hips and down one leg. And when he was through, he sighed and settled her entrance right above the head of his cock. She'd never had sex like this, backward and on a lap, but she trembled with the excitement of being with him again.

Positioned over him, she lowered down and took half of his length, then eased off with a moan. Kirk tensed under her and let off a soft, rumbling noise from his chest. He brushed his hand over the outer edge of her tattoos, then gripped her waist hard again and pushed her back over his dick. With his knees, he spread hers wider and slid into her again, deeper.

"Oh, my gosh," she whispered at the intense sensation. Nothing had ever felt like this before.

Kirk set the pace with one hand, dragging her waist against him as he moved inside of her, and with his other brushed up her ribs and cupped her breast. With a gasp, she closed her eyes and bowed against his touch. Slowly, he pulled her back against his chest, and clamped his teeth over her shoulder, hard enough to burn but not break the skin.

*Against the law...*
*Fuck a law that would strip rights...*
*Want to be with him...*
*Only him...*
*Teeth, teeth, teeth, gentle kiss...*
*Toaso...*

"Kirk," she gasped out breathlessly as he moved within her, pushing her closer to climax with every stroke.

He sucked hard on her skin, and she could feel them now. Sharp teeth. Too sharp. Elongating. Kirk dragged them against her skin, and now the light was too bright, the sound of the waterfall was too loud, the sound of her pounding heartbeat deafening. She clutched onto his hand as he massaged her breast, desperate to keep him tight against her because she was falling. Her stomach dipped into the water, and she arched her neck back and cried out as her ecstasy intensified. "Please," she whimpered, her skin lifting in chills under his teasing bite. "Claim me."

The pain was instant, warring with the first pulse of an orgasm that seized her entire body. Deep throbbing pulses of pleasure drummed against resonating fire that sparked at the nerve endings in her shoulder. His teeth drove into her easily, so sharp, four puncture wounds that drew a wince from her.

Kirk released her skin and pulled her against him so hard it left her breathless. He bucked into her fast, and his body was hard as stone. He rested his forehead against the back of her neck and gritted out her name as his dick throbbed inside of her. Warm, so warm. Kirk grunted a sexy, out of control sound as he rammed into her again and shot more heat into her. Powerful legs, abs going rock hard against her back, arm so tight around her, like he never wanted to let go. And now he didn't have to.

She was claimed.

As her orgasm pulsed on, encouraged by his own release, she smiled in potent relief.

Fuck what she'd been through and where

she came from. Fuck all her mistakes. This right here was the moment she would be better, because now she had a reason. Kirk deserved a mate who was whole and strong, not broken and feeble. And what an empowering experience to be picked by a man like him. Strong, capable, dominant silverback shifter who could've had anyone in the world. And for whatever reason, he'd sifted through her rough edges and found her good parts. He'd seen his future in her.

Kirk made her feel normal, cared for, and safe.

Safe.

That word had meant nothing to her before she'd met him, and now she understood. It was warmth, security, and confidence. It was walking through the flames of loneliness and being shielded from the burn by the man she adored. It was relaxing into the idea that the other shoe wasn't going to drop. That the bad was over and done. That she'd paid her dues and now she was bathing in the reward. That if she fell asleep against him, she would wake up whole and shielded from the grit of the outside world.

Caring for the injury he'd caused her, Kirk ran his tongue over the four puncture wounds on her shoulder. It was an animalistic need to take care of her, and she loved it. He hadn't said it yet, but Kirk loved her too.

Now, neither of them had to be scared because they were bound.

Let the law try to take this away from them.

She would bring hell to earth to protect what she and Kirk had found.

# TWELVE

Alison came out of the river waves on legs that were so wobbly they didn't want to hold her upright anymore.

Claimed. She was Kirk's claim. A wave of joy and excitement washed over her.

Kirk turned in front of her, tall as an oak, strong and steadfast as a mountain. Every muscle rippled on his body as he lifted his hand toward her. And his eyes...yellow flames, glowing from the pupils out.

"You never hide him from me," she murmured, feeling numb.

"Never felt the need to with you."

She slid her hand against his palm and allowed him to help her slog through the sand to her clothes. As she dressed, he watched her with a slight frown marring his dark brows.

"What are you thinking?"

Kirk shook his head like he would shut down again, but when he reached for his jeans, he said, "I never knew how Kong did it."

"Did what?"

His lips ticked up, then fell too fast for the smile to reach his eyes. Gaze averted, he said, "I lived with him, Layla, and Josephine for a while. I had to. Kong needed his family group close. I could see it was good for him. He talks..." Kirk ghosted a glance up to Alison and tried again. "He talks easy. Much easier than me, and I would just watch him with Layla. He was open, and it was good for her. It made her happy. She knows everything about him."

"I don't understand," Alison murmured, tugging the hem of her shirt into place.

Kirk strangled his sandy T-shirt and straightened his spine, then leveled her with that blazing gaze of his. "I should've waited to mark you. I should've waited until you knew everything."

Her heart stuttered and ached in her chest cavity. "You regret claiming me?"

"No." He huffed and shook his head. "But you will."

Feeling like someone had just socked her in the stomach, she gritted out, "I'm pretty sure I won't."

"I'm not a good person—"

"Neither am I, Kirk!" Stupid tears burned her eyes, but she blinked them away.

Lightning flashed in the distance behind him as he watched her with an utterly baffled expression on his face, but hang it all, he was ruining this. And hang her if she let him see her cry. "I can't even believe you're doing this." Alison strode for the woods, dashing her knuckles under her eyes just to make sure those fuckin' tears stayed in place as anger, hurt, and sorrow pulsed through her veins.

"What am I doing wrong now?"

"Shutting down on me. Again! It's what you do, right?" Alison tripped on a root and went down hard, but an instant before she hit the ground, Kirk was there, his arm wrapped around her waist. He set her upright. She shoved off him and screamed a furious sound. She didn't want to be saved right now. "You push and pull and push again. And you tease me with these beautiful moments, and then retract them an instant later."

"I'm trying to tell you I don't talk easy, but I want to with you!"

She crossed her arms and winced at the pain on her shoulder.

He was to her in a flash, pulling at her

shirt, exposing the puncture wounds he'd made. "You hurt different than me."

"What does that even mean?"

"It means I'm used to pain, and I hate seeing you hurt. I did that to you."

Her shoulders sagged, and she sucked air through her tightening vocal cords. "Kirk, can't you see? This," she struggled to say as she gestured to her claiming mark, "felt like the best thing that ever happened to me. You telling me I'll regret being bound to you hurts worse than any torn skin ever could. I wanted you to let me keep that feeling."

Kirk shifted his weight from side to side, backing away from her slowly. "What feeling?"

"Happy. Safe. Loved. Chosen despite my faults. All of it. You are ice, Kirk."

"What do you mean?"

"I can hold you in my hand and I think I'm keeping you. I *feel* you. But all the while you are melting and slipping through my fingers."

He swallowed hard and looked sick. Eyes on the woods, he hooked his hands on his hips and shook his head for a long time. His nostrils flared slightly in the moment before he spoke. "I don't want to be ice. Not anymore. Not with you. Bash told me once I need to pick a person to let in." Kirk dragged his gaze to hers. "I always thought if I did that—if I let someone see all of me—they would run."

"I'm not running."

"But what if—"

"Kirk." Alison stepped over the pine needle covered forest floor and pulled his hands from his hips, gripped them hard. "I'm. Not. Running."

"I panicked a little," he admitted low.

"Yeah, it sucked."

Kirk ran his hands through his damp hair and linked his fingers behind his head. Chin held high, he looked down at her with a calculating look. "You want to see me?"

"Yes," she said, void of hesitation. "No more hot and cold." She twitched her head toward her right shoulder where her seeping claiming mark burned on. "I'm yours now. You picked me as your person when you bit me. Now let me the fuck in."

His inhumanly bright eyes crinkled at the corners with his smile. "Okay," he said, as if he'd just accepted a dare. Kirk shocked her when he threw her over his shoulder like a sack of mulch. "You asked for it."

She yelped as he smacked her ass. "Kirk Slater, I'm not just some cavewoman you can drag anywhere you want. We're having a fight.

There are rules."

"Don't care much for rules. Admission one," he said as he stomped onto the beach and toward the thin trail up the side of the falls. "When I was seven, I stole all of my half-brother, Aaron's, baseball cards, because he was a huge douchebag, and I blamed it on my other half-brother, Byron, who was also a douchebag. And then they got in this huge, bloody fight on the front lawn of my house, and my dad got involved, and I still don't feel guilty."

"On account of them being douchebags?"

"Yep. Age ten I met a human girl in town while my mom was shopping, and when she asked where I was from, I told her Lowland Gap. She told me it was a commune for a cult, and I called her a titty-witch. I didn't know what a commune or a cult was, so I snuck into my dad's office when we got back to the house and researched it on the computer. It sounded pretty damn familiar, so I ran away from home."

"How far did you make it?"

"Well, since I only packed three pair of underwear and five beef jerky sticks, not far, and my dad tanned my hide when he found me."

"None of this makes me want to leave."

"Give it time. Age eleven, the blackback in me started wanting to fight. So I did. I fought everyone, all the damned time. I even went after my dad, a fully mature silverback, a time or two."

Alison let her arms go limp as they bumped and bounced across Kirk's bare, flexing, sexy as hell back. "What's a blackback?"

"A young male gorilla. I started fighting early and pissed off everyone in my cult."

"Don't call it that."

"A cult is what it was, Ally. You should know that. Accept it. I wasn't raised like you, or the Boarlanders, or even Kong. His mom took him away from their family group. Sho raised him in regular schools with humans. I only knew my family for the first half of my life."

They were really high up now, so Alison closed her eyes against the dizzying height. "My mom used to get high before we went grocery shopping. She would be leaning against buildings as we walked there, and I'd have to hold her upright and make sure she kept up with her purse. I was in charge of getting groceries while she would be sagging against the shopping cart."

"How old when it started?"

"I don't know. I remember being really young when I started being embarrassed of her in public. Six maybe?"

"Jesus." Kirk crested the top of the steep incline and settled her on her feet.

"My point is your unconventional upbringing isn't a deal-breaker for me. Now tell me more confessions. I like this."

Squaring up to her, he tucked her short hair behind her ear. "You like what?"

"Knowing you. It makes you feel more like home."

Kirk huffed a disbelieving laugh and searched her eyes. He gritted his teeth, then said, "That's because I haven't told you the bad stuff yet."

Alison slid her arms around his waist and hugged him tight. "You won't scare me off."

"No," he rumbled. Kirk kissed the top of her head and murmured, "I can't imagine much scares you anymore." He turned her slowly in his hands and gripped her uninjured shoulder as he faced her toward the storm.

For miles Alison could see rolling mountains covered in a blur of green and brown, and in the distance, the storm clouds created a wall of dark gray. The deep rumble of thunder echoed across Damon's mountains, and she leaned her back against Kirk's chest as she took in the beauty of the place.

"This is part of me," he murmured low, his cheek resting against her temple.

Her shoulder hurt with him pressed against her, but she maintained a straight face and didn't grimace away from his touch because this was an important moment.

"I come up here when my head gets messed up. And when Clinton is pissin' me off and I want to murder him. This is where I come when the guilt gets too bad and I can't control my Changes."

"Why guilt?" she whispered, her heart breaking with his admission.

"I signed a contract. One that said I wouldn't have sex with women, just in case Fiona called me up to head a family group. I didn't want to sign it, not because I wanted to have sex, but because she was a new leader and had been killing off her opposition. I'd already slept with a couple women and didn't like signing away something that belonged to me. I wanted to choose my family group and have them choose me, too. I denied her, and at the time, I was working in town, away from my family group because I was getting too dominant to stay in the same place as my dad. She had me taken and beaten until I signed it."

"Oh, my gosh. How long did it take?"

"Three days." He sighed. "I was to guard Kong with another silverback named Rhett. He didn't have to be broken. He signed it willingly. I don't know why. Maybe he thought he would be assigned a family group later or something, but I could see what was happening for what it was. We were being broken, like she'd done to her personal guards. I was there when they brought Kong in. She made me watch because he was going to be mine to keep in line. He was tortured for three weeks, and I was chained in the corner because I tried to stop it. Mona thought it would be good for me to watch. She thought it would desensitize me. Rhett helped them break him, and then he helped bring in Kong's mom, Josephine, and Kong finally gave in." Kirk swallowed hard. "In those three weeks, something went hollow in my middle. All I smelled was blood, sweat, and pain. Something died inside of me, or got erased, I don't know. I stopped feeling. I was telling Kong to just sign the contract so we could both escape that place, but he had been raised outside of our people, and he wanted a single mate. He wanted to keep his old life. And by the end, I was hoping he would stop breathing because...shit." Kirk slipped away from her and stood five feet back, out of reach, like he didn't want her touching him when he told her what he'd been through. "I was hoping he would stop breathing because I could see both of our futures, and they were empty. He would be saved for a massive family group. He would fuck them mindlessly when they went into heat, give all of himself to provide for them, and he would never connect with another living creature. Not really. And I would help keep his life dark. He'd known freedom. He'd been away from our people, and his mom had raised him in a loving environment. I only knew a half-life, and to get him back to accepting our fucked-up peoples' ways, he would have to be dead inside, just like me. And I thought maybe if he just stopped living, it would be the easy way out. But he didn't, and for the next several years, I limped along beside him, watching him wither, watching him pine for Layla, watching Rhett make his life a living hell. I was part of the torture, Ally."

A soft, heartbroken sound eked from her throat. He looked wary of touch still, and his eyes were a light gold color now, so she sat and faced the storm clouds and waited. After a couple of minutes, Kirk sat beside her.

"When did you stop working for Fiona?"

Kirk drew his knees up and draped his arms over them as he stared at the lightning in the distance. "The day she told me and Rhett we needed to kill Layla's guardian, Mac. He was old. In hospice care. And Fiona was pissed over the information Rhett had been feeding her about Kong sneaking off to be with Layla. Fiona wanted to hurt Kong by hurting his mate. And nothing could've hurt Layla more than the death of Mac. I couldn't do it, though. I'd had enough. My survival instinct had been strong until then, but when we got to that point, I couldn't hurt Kong. I couldn't hurt Layla. When I told Fiona I was going rogue, she said she was going to kill me, and I believed her. With every cell in my body, I knew my days were numbered."

"What happened to Layla's guardian?"

Kirk's lips pressed into a thin line, and he leveled her a vacant look.

"Rhett killed him, didn't he?" she asked in a horrified whisper.

Kirk's Adam's apple dipped low as his gaze dropped to the ground. "I went to his funeral.

Layla and Kong forgive me for it all. They're good like that, but I still go put flowers on Mac's grave. He was a good man, and my people ended his life just to hurt someone else. Gorilla shifters, they don't care about human life like they should. Fiona trained them not to. She convinced them they're a superior species who should just take what they want."

"Do you talk to your family anymore?"

"Fuck no. I'm a traitor in their eyes, and that's fine by me. I don't regret leaving them behind."

She was quiet for a long time, mulling that over. Kirk said it so flippantly, like his family group meant nothing to him now, but she knew better. "I used to beg my mom to stay straight for me. Beg and beg and beg. And she would change for a few days. A week. Maybe two, and I would get in this endless cycle where I believed her because I wanted so badly to feel like I was important enough for her to change and be better. And each time she failed me, I was cut deeper." Alison scooted closer to Kirk and rested her head on his shoulder. "She was no good, but it didn't change me wishing that she was. It hurts, tearing your heart away from the people who you are supposed to love the most, Kirk. It

151

hurts for always."

Eyes on the storm, Kirk heaved a sigh and nodded. "Yeah."

"It makes it hard to let people in."

Another nod. Kirk picked up a rock and chucked it into the river that was tumbling over the cliff ledge in front of them. "I was doing a bang up job until I came to work for the Boarlanders." He chuckled darkly. "And then you came along and filled my hollow parts and now I can't stop *feeling*. It's annoying."

She giggled and clamped her teeth over his arm, then rested her chin on it and looked up at him. "Ugh, feelings. So gross."

"So gross," he agreed, but he was smiling now.

"I still don't regret it, just so you know."

Kirk's gaze drifted to her shoulder. "Does it still hurt?"

"Like hellfire."

"You heal ridiculously slowly."

"Yeah," she said, shoving him back until he lay on the ground. "Being human is such a drag." She straddled his stomach and grinned down at him.

He slid his hands up her thighs and narrowed his eyes. "This is the part where

152

you're supposed to be scrambling back down the trail to escape me."

"Yeah, I chopped up bricks of coke in a dank room completely naked for two years. Sorry, babe. I don't scare easily."

"Mm. So you know, I'm going to have to fight more now."

"Why?"

The smile dipped from his face, and then returned slowly. "Because you're my family group now."

"And your instincts tell you to keep in tip-top shape to protect me?"

He dipped his chin to his chest. "That's right."

"You know I can protect myself, right?"

"I do. My gorilla doesn't care about that stuff, though. It's ingrained in me."

"Why are you smiling like that?"

"Because A—fucking you under the falls was awesome. B—you asked me to claim you, and C—I thought maybe this part of me would've been broken after what happened with Fiona. I was afraid watching Kong get tortured had killed my protective instincts. And maybe it did for a while but now everything is different. I would do anything to keep you safe and happy, because I feel normal around you. And for me, that's a really big deal."

"You feel like a normal silverback gorilla man."

"Yep."

She snickered and splayed her hands against his taut chest, locking her arms against him. "You've turned me into a criminal, you know."

"Breaking the law," he drawled, though he didn't look guilty at all. "We can keep your mark to ourselves if you want."

She fingered the healing skin of her bite on his chest. "I think we have to. They can arrest you if they know you've claimed me. And they won't put you in some solitary confinement cell, Kirk. They'll put you somewhere they can make an example of you. Somewhere you'll be targeted by other inmates. I can't be the reason you get hurt. I need you here with me."

He drew her palm to his lips and kissed her gently. "Say that last part again."

"Kirk, I'm serious. We could get in huge trouble—"

"Woman, I knew the risks going into this. I was forced to sign a damned abstinence contract and work a job I hated, and now I'm being forced to give up on claiming you? At some point I have to do what I want and say fuck everyone trying to run my life. It's me and you now. We'll keep our marks hidden and share the secret, just me and you. And when yours heals... probably in ten years, because look at that," he said, brushing his fingertips near her shoulder and holding up his red-stained hand. "You're still bleeding."

She swatted his hand away.

"When your mark heals," he continued, "it'll be hidden by your tattoos. Someone will have to look pretty damn hard to catch us."

"You got a claiming mark!" Bash yelled.

"Aw, shit," Kirk muttered, sitting up quick and shielding her from the grinning titan who had just poked his head up from the cliff trail.

"Guys, I found them, and Clinton, you were wrong. They aren't fucking gorilla-style! They're cuddling, and she has a claiming mark!" Bash's voice echoed across the mountains.

No, no, no!

Alison scrambled to pull the thin strap of her tank top over her puncture wounds as Bash climbed up the trail and turned to give Emerson a hand up.

"Bash," Kirk rushed out in a hiss. "Keep your voice down. She isn't supposed to have one."

"Oh, yeah," Bash said, slamming a big blue cooler down next to them. "The cops told us no claiming. But you're the cop," Bash said, eyebrows arched high. "That's funny. Boarlanders got a cop mate now." The dark-headed bear shifter frowned. "Or the Lowlanders. Does this mean I get to play with your gun?"

"Uuuh," Alison said, "no."

"Damn."

Emerson was holding a small video camera pointed at Alison and Kirk as she sank into her mate's lap and said, "I'm doing videos of our crew for when our baby gets older. I'm documenting everything so Bash and I can do a video documentary for memories. We suck at scrapbooking." Emerson panned to the tumbling river in front of them. "Nice place. You ever jumped off the falls?"

Alison felt silly straddling Kirk's lap now, but when she tried to move off him, he held her tighter. "I have a boner," he gritted out with a significant look.

"I have a boner, too," Bash said as he pulled a bottle of beer from the cooler. "I mean, I always have a boner now that Emerson is around because her tits are soft and bounce around real nice—"

"That's good, Bash Bear," Emerson said through a giggle as she cupped his cheek.

"But I was just telling them my dick gets even harder now that you're pregnant."

"You're pregnant?" Alison asked.

"Yeah, and it isn't against the law," Emerson said defensively.

"No, no. I'm not getting you in trouble. Congratulations!"

Under her, Kirk's boner was getting harder and bigger. Him using her to cover it up wasn't helping.

Bash handed her a beer. "Since you're wicked and unlawful now, you and Kirk should have tons of babies. Fuck in ten-ten if you want to get instant pregnant. I'll babysit."

"Oh, God," Kirk muttered, hugging her tighter against his chest.

"You smell like blood and sex," Bash said, right before he took a long swig of his drink. "I like your dove tattoo on your side boob."

Alison buried her face against Kirk's chest as her cheeks burned with mortification.

Emerson helped zero percent. She was just sitting in her mate's lap, laughing.

"What does it mean?" Kirk asked, looking at it sideways as she scrambled to pull the low hanging sleeve hole over to cover her skin better. She regretted not putting her bra back on.

Horrified, she whispered, "It's a reminder to see the good in people."

Kirk's eyes jerked to hers, and a slow, heart-stopping smile stretched his lips. "I like that. What about that one?" He pointed to the sails of a pirate ship that took up most of her ribcage.

Self-conscious, she hung her head and cast Bash and Emerson a shy glance. No way could she muster the courage to explain them to anyone other than Kirk, much less on camera. "I don't really show these to people."

"Well, why not?" Bash asked.

"I guess because I'm kind of messed up, and these tell my story."

"You ain't messed up," Bash said with a shake of his head. He pointed to Harrison, who had just crested the trail. "He's messed up. I'm messed up." He pointed his beer bottle back to the woods, where a still drunk and swaying Clinton was leaning heavily against a tree. "He's super messed up."

"I'm normal," Mason called from down the trail.

Bash shook his head and lowered his

voice. "No he ain't. Point is we're all messed up. You look pretty damn normal to me. You and Kirk both."

Huh.

"You think Kirk is normal and I'm not?" Clinton slurred. "You're an ass...butt."

"Good one, Clinton," Harrison said as he sat on Kirk's other side.

"I think I'm going to puke," Clinton groaned.

When Harrison leaned back on locked arms and narrowed his eyes on Alison, the air suddenly felt too heavy to breathe. "Nice claiming mark."

Clinton fell with a thud onto the ground behind them, rested his hands on his stomach, and glared up at the sky. "She'll be the death of us all now. Bye bye Boarlanders."

Emerson glared at him. "You're exhausting."

"Good job, Kirk," Clinton mumbled. "You claimed a grenade."

"What does that mean?" Alison asked. She was trying real hard not to get offended, but this guy was being a jerk.

"You still think you're here to keep the peace, don't you?"

"Yes," she gritted out, "because I am."

Clinton started fake snoring. Everyone stared at him for a moment, then Bash went back to passing out beers, and Mason sat down next to Clinton's limp body.

"Hey, remember that time you claimed the woman who shot you?" Mason asked.

"Dude," Kirk said with a frown for the dark-haired behemoth sitting behind him.

"I'm just pointing out that Bash said you're the normal one of the group, which clearly is not the case."

"Does everyone know I shot you?" Alison asked.

Kirk said, "No," at the same time everyone else said, "Yes."

Fantastic.

"I don't like weapons in my territory," Harrison said in a dark, gravelly voice.

Her stomach dipped to her toes, and slowly, she turned around and settled on the ground between Kirk's legs. "I owe you an apology. Lots of them, actually. I didn't know what you and Georgia had been through. I was just doing what I was trained to do, but my partner and I should've taken the time to come in slow and easy. It wasn't the first impression I had hoped to make on you, and I won't bring my weapon into your territory anymore out of respect for what you've been through."

"Isn't that dangerous for you, being here unprotected?" There was a sarcastic edge to the alpha's voice.

Eyes on another lightning flash over the mountains, Alison huffed a breath and shook her head. "I don't think my Glock would protect me from much here. And besides, I don't feel like I need it anymore when I'm up here." She shrugged her shoulder up to her ear. "I have Kirk, and none of you seem to want to hurt me."

"I do," Clinton said.

"Hurt her, and I'll kill you," Kirk said nonchalantly as he brushed his fingers down the dove tattoo.

When Alison turned to look at Clinton around Kirk's shoulder, Mason was glaring down at him with a calculating look. "I could suffocate him if you want me to, Boss Bear."

"Let him be," Harrison ground out. "Officer Holman, Kirk ain't mine to worry about. He's Kong's. That and he's a grown-ass man who can make his own decision on who he chooses for a mate." He turned a lightened gaze on her. "I hope you'll excuse me for pointing out the obvious, but you feel scary. That mark on your shoulder is illegal now, and you're a human cop. I don't want him hurt."

"I don't either, and I understand your concern. We're going to hide it, though. I won't hurt him. I won't hurt any of you." She leveled the alpha a look and let him see the honesty in her eyes when she whispered, "I promise."

# THIRTEEN

Alison liked the Boarlanders.

They'd sat up above the falls for an hour teasing and laughing and cutting up as they watched the storm pass. Even when it had started sprinkling on them, no one moved to get up. And little by little, Harrison had relaxed beside her.

Kirk had gone completely affectionate, cuddling her, stroking her, kissing the back of her neck and around her claiming mark in between talking to the others, almost as if he didn't notice he was doing it.

Something had changed between them since they'd made love under the falls. Or perhaps that change had come about because they'd opened up to each other afterward, or because they'd claimed each other, she didn't know. All she knew was she'd never felt this

163

sure of anyone, or this happy.

"I'm glad I'm not the only human in the crew anymore," Emerson said, cradling her still flat stomach.

Kirk nibbled Alison's earlobe and smiled against her. "I'm glad, too. I thought there was no way in hell a woman like her would ever settle for a man like me."

"Now that's just stupid," Bash said. "There ain't nothin' wrong with you, and love don't work like that. Emerson's the smartest woman on the planet, and she picked me."

"She ain't that smart then," Clinton grumbled.

"Go jump off a cliff," Mason said.

"Okay." Clinton stood up and sauntered to the edge, right beside the falls. "I'm gonna do it, and I'll probably die, and y'all will miss me when I'm gone."

"No, don't do it," Kirk said half-heartedly.

Clinton narrowed his eyes at all of them, gave them the bird with both hands, and launched himself off the edge.

A few seconds later, there was a huge splash below them.

"Is he dead?" Mason asked, making his way to the ledge.

"I jump from here all the time," Kirk

muttered. "We can't get rid of him that easily."

"Still alive," Clinton taunted them from below.

"See?" Kirk said. He swung his attention to Alison, and now there was a mischievous glint in his eyes. "Hold your nose."

"What?" Alison asked, startled.

Kirk was grinning now and looked pure wicked. "Hold your nose!"

He launched upward, taking her with him in a tight embrace, then jumped from the falls. Alison screamed bloody murder as her stomach lodged in her throat and tried to escape her body, and at the last, heart-pounding second, she sucked in a breath and pinched her nose. And oh, that river stung her skin, but underwater, her anger evaporated as she opened her eyes. Kirk was there smiling like a maniac, and around them, the other Boarlanders were dropping into the water, surrounded by millions of tiny bubbles that raced toward the surface.

Kirk shoved her toward the surface with a surprising amount of strength, and she broke the waves with a gasp. "Monster!" she yelped as he bit her ass on his way up.

He treaded water as the others came up for air. Unashamedly, he said, "I can see your nipples through your shirt now."

"We should call Audrey and ask her to bring home barbecue," Bash called from where he bobbed in the water. "You should have a claiming party."

"You just want an excuse to throw a party," Clinton muttered as he swam by like a grumpy frog.

"No, I don't. Claiming is a big deal. Ally is one of us now."

"No, Bash," Harrison said. "She'll be a Lowlander claim."

Kirk's smile faded as he watched the Boarlander alpha swim toward shore.

Something about the hurt in his expression slashed pain through Alison's stomach. The decision to stay or go back to Kong wasn't just hurting Kirk, she realized. The uncertainty was hurting all of them.

She kissed his neck because she was a coward. It hurt too much to see that pain in his eyes. He rubbed her back gently, then pushed her toward shore. She understood his need for action. She didn't like people seeing her hurt either.

Up on the sandy beach though, Harrison cursed loud enough for it to echo through the valley. He linked his hands behind his head, then turned slowly. His eyes were blazing bright blue, and he looked as gutted as Kirk did. "I'm sorry, man. My bear got set off when Officer Holman and her partner came charging into our woods, and I'm spiraling, but it's no excuse. I'm happy you found her. Happy you found the one. I'll call Audrey and ask her to bring back food tonight, and we'll celebrate it right. Legality be damned, this is a really big deal."

Alison dragged her feet through the waves and did her best to cover her tits with her crossed arms. Her thin, soaking wet shirt wasn't doing her any favors as Kirk guided her up toward the sandy beach, his hand on her lower back.

"Harrison," Kirk said, "I know you don't get the draw, but she's been calling to my gorilla since that first night in the woods. She came into our territory, all fierce looking, gun pulled, here to save Emerson, but that was the moment for me. I was Changed, and my animal drew up short on a woman for the first time ever. My animal picked, and I tried to fight it. She tried to fight it, too. I did my best not to call her, to leave her alone, but I only lasted a day and a half and it hurt us both. It felt like ripping my own guts out being away from her.

You know fighting a pairing doesn't work."

"I know," Harrison murmured. With a sigh, he stuck out a hand to Alison. "Harrison Lang, alpha of the Boarlanders."

Okay, they were starting over, and she was glad for it, but she was also wearing a soaking wet shirt. She squeaked and shook his hand fast, then covered back up. "Alison Holman, but I would really like it if you called me Ally instead of Officer Holman. I'm off duty."

"She said doody," Bash said with a snicker, and up the beach, hiking down the trail toward them, Emerson giggled.

Harrison's face cracked into a grin, and he snorted. Shaking his head, he took off for the woods and called over his shoulder, "Come on, Bash Bear. We have a claiming party to throw together. Ally, welcome to the C-Team."

# FOURTEEN

"What did Harrison mean by C-Team?" Alison asked, holding on tighter around Kirk's neck as he carried her on his back through Boarlander woods. Her flip-flops dangled from her fingers and bounced against his chest with every step he took.

"C-Team used to be a Gray Back thing. They were wild. Still are, but the mates in Grayland Mobile Park have at least got them settled enough to hit their lumber numbers. But before Mason and I came to help out, Harrison lost a lot of his crew, and they fell way behind on their work."

"How did he lose his crew?"

"Clinton."

He didn't offer more explanation than that, so she asked, "So they are the C-Team because the Boarlanders don't hit their numbers?"

169

"Yeah, but we will dig ourselves out of C-Team status if we can just get through a damned week without fightin'."

"But you said you'll need to fight more now."

"Not like this. Clinton is convinced ladies in the trailer park are some kind of jinx. He was really bad before Audrey battled for her place here. He has bounced from crew to crew, and it ain't the crews' faults he can't adjust. His head is a mess, and his bear matches. I know he hurt your feelings back there, but trust me when I say he has been downright tame about you being in the trailer park. About you being claimed."

"That does make me feel a little better. I thought he just hated me."

Kirk snorted. "He hates everyone on the outside. On the inside, though, he feels more than he lets on. Most days, you'll want to shoot his ass. But he'll have one day in ten where he does something that makes him seem almost...redeemable."

"You're wrong, asshole," Clinton said as he strode around them. "I ain't redeemable, fuck you very much."

Kirk didn't even flinch at the vitriol in his voice. The muscled, sandy blond-haired man stomped away in front of them but slowed, then stopped. He turned, his eyes sparking with anger, but he dropped his gaze to the ground and growled, "You hear him?"

"Who?" Kirk asked.

Clinton jerked his light gray eyes to Alison, then back to the ground. "You should cover up your mark." He hesitated another moment, then spun and strode off down the trail toward the trailer park.

Kirk set her down immediately and backed her into the brush behind a thick trunk of an Aspen. He peeled off his shirt. "Here, put this on," he murmured low, checking the trail around the tree.

"What's happening?"

"Someone's yelling up ahead. Sounds like your partner."

"Shit," she whispered as she struggled into his light gray, oversize shirt. It hung down to her knees. Finn could not find out about her mark. She had only known him for a couple of weeks, but he was anti-shifter, plain as day. And if he was a by-the-book cop, he would turn her into their superiors the moment he saw her claiming mark, no matter that they were partners. And she had no doubt in her mind that law enforcement would make an example of them. It would be the first shifter offense they enforced. She and Kirk could both be locked up.

"Holman!" Finn yelled through the woods.

Kirk cupped her cheeks and lifted his brows as he leveled her a look. "It'll be okay. I promise I won't let anything happen to you." He leaned down and kissed her, pushed his tongue past her lips once, then disengaged and rested his forehead against hers. "You feel different."

She closed her eyes and sighed as a feeling of utter safety slipped over her again. With a smile, she whispered, "So do you."

"Holman!"

She let off a human growl and made her way back to the trail. Finn was coming in and fast. Harrison followed at a distance, his eyes wild and blue, and his jaw clenched. Up ahead, Clinton squatted down, stripping pine needles off a branch, his body placed between Alison and her pissed-off looking partner.

"Close enough," Clinton barked out.

"It's okay, Clinton," she said, squeezing his shoulder as she passed. "What are you doing here?" she asked Finn.

His mouth flopped open, and his face turned red, the color of his hair. "Are you fucking kidding me? What am I doing here? What are *you* doing here? And in that?" He waved to her giant T-shirt. "This is against the rules!"

"What rules?"

"You know…fraternizing with…with…"

"The enemy? They aren't an enemy. We're supposed to be working beside them, and I'm off-duty. Who I choose to hang out with in my downtime is my choice."

"But they're…"

"They're what? Shifters? I know you weren't about to say suspects or criminals. *Know* you weren't. They haven't done anything wrong."

"So killing an entire government agency isn't doing anything wrong?"

"No proof," Clinton said blandly.

"Are you talking about IESA?" she asked. "The undercover government agency that went rogue? The agency that got their dumb asses videotaped by Cora Keller and exposed to the world because of their messy assassination attempts? The agency not even the government will publicly claim? Sorry Finn, but your assumptions about these people were wrong. If IESA agents are missing, it's because the shifters up here were defending

173

themselves."

"Which should be brought to light in court to see who is really guilty."

"A trial the government would never let see the light of day, Finn! They aren't dragging IESA out to expose all the illegal, unethical, horrible shit they did! If the IESA met their end here, the shifters did the government a damned favor."

"And again, no proof," Kirk said. His voice had cooled. "I don't recall any IESA agents storming these mountains. Don't remember them trying to wipe out every shifter here. Don't remember them coming after innocent men, women, and children. Don't remember them raising some of the people here in a tooting facility, torturing kids, running experiments, scarring the survivors. That's all rumors and hearsay." Kirk's voice had gone hollow, as if he didn't care if Finn believed him or not. "If you want to back the attempted massacre of an entire species, probably do that somewhere else so you don't get your heart plucked from your chest here."

With every word Kirk had spoken, Alison had grown sicker and sicker. Testing facilities? That hadn't even been mentioned in Cora Keller's attack on the agency. The shifters here had gone through so much more than she, or likely anyone else, realized. And yet here they were, accepting her as Kirk's claim, even though she was human.

Finn was so wrong in his assumption that the shifters were the bad guys.

"My mate is bringing home barbecue later, and we're gonna have some beer and throw some horseshoes if you want to stay and join us," Harrison gritted out. "Since you are working right alongside of us, it might benefit you to get to know us, like Ally is doing."

"You mean Officer Holman," Finn ground out, his eyes narrowed on the alpha.

"No, I mean Ally. She's a friend here and plenty welcome to spend time in Damon's mountains to do her job because she made the effort to get to know us and secure that open invite. You still don't have Damon's permission to be on his land unescorted, so if you want the same privileges Ally has, you should make more of an effort to get us to trust you. Sitting up in your little cabin glaring at us as we drive by isn't gonna do you any favors."

Finn had donned his uniform to come up here, and he crossed his arms over his chest as he inhaled deeply, eyes on her. "Look, Holman, I'm your partner. You know what it's like to lose a partner, don't you?"

Alison closed her eyes against the pain of the memory of Riggs gasping for air on the floor. "Yeah." Her voice cracked on the word.

"Well, you're my partner, and I've called you ten damned times."

"My phone is sitting in the front seat of the truck."

"Great, but can you see why I was worried? Last I saw, you were fishtailing out of our post, headed for these mountains, and you didn't call me for backup, but you also didn't pick up the phone to let me know you were all right."

And now she felt like shit. "I'm really sorry. It didn't work like that undercover. It was every man for himself, and I didn't think about your side of it."

"Well, next time call me and let me know what you're doing so I don't just sit down there thinking you're up here bleeding out or something." He cast a quick narrow-eyed glance to Harrison. "And no, I don't want a beer."

Harrison pursed his lips and nodded. "Then you'll have to get out of my territory." With a quick flick of his fingers, he gestured Finn back toward the trailer park.

Kirk gripped Alison's waist and gave her a

quick kiss on the side of the head as they followed the others through the woods. Finn narrowed his eyes at them but was smart enough to keep his mouth shut. Partner or not, he had no say in who she dated.

"You look ridiculous and completely unprofessional," he grumbled as she stepped into line with him.

"We went swimming at the falls," Kirk said in a deep, rough tone. "It ain't like she's naked."

Finn offered him a dirty look, then sighed and arced his attention to Alison. "Look, I get the draw. It's lonely as fuck up here. Why do you think I'm always down in Saratoga? But you aren't even wearing your damned badge."

"Finn, I'm not cut from the same cloth as you. You worked in a precinct with rules, dress codes, and organization. That was never my work environment. If I wore a badge, it would've gotten me shot, and my dress code was street clothes because a uniform would—"

"Get you shot. Yeah, I get it. I've worked around undercover cops, you know? They would come into our precinct every once in a while, dressed down, inconspicuous, but you could always tell by their eyes they weren't just someone there to report a crime. They all had that haunted, hard look. I made you as an undercover cop the second I saw you at the airport."

"You did not."

"I swear I did. Also when I tried to look you up in the system, I could barely find anything on you. I had to ask around Chicago to get the scoop on you."

"Had to," she muttered sarcastically.

"This wasn't my choice either, you know? I was used to being on the streets, and then I came to play shifter babysitter up in the wilderness with a partner I knew nothing about." Finn shook his head.

"What did you learn about her?" Kirk asked.

"Ha!" Finn gave him a pointed look. "I see those fuckin' lovey dovey looks you're giving her, but don't be fooled. She's a pit viper."

"And yet somehow that makes her more attractive to me," Kirk murmured.

Finn snorted. "Shifters. You know what they used to call her?"

"Finn, shut up." Alison didn't know why he was so damned talkative all the sudden. He'd come in here pissed off, and now he was a Chatty-Cathy. She was seriously stifling the urge to punch him in the mouth-hole right now.

"What did they call her?" Clinton asked from behind them.

"Ghost."

Mother fucker, whoever he'd tracked down to dish dirt on her was going to get an earful from her.

"Why Ghost?" Mason asked from where he leaned on the corner of a trailer as they came out of the tree line.

"Because she was quiet. They say she could blend in anywhere, melt through walls."

"I thought you just worked in that drug house," Kirk said, confusion in his voice.

"In Chicago?" Finn asked, tossing her a wicked glare. "Nah. She worked for years undercover before that, changing her hair, changing her name, living where they told her to with no complaints. She thrived. A real chameleon. She made a dent in drug trafficking wherever they assigned her. Cartels, drug lords, dealers...no one even know what hit 'em." Finn crossed his arms as they came to a stop on the edge of the evening shadows stretching from the trees. "I almost didn't believe my sources because you don't make any sense. Too soft spoken. Not the right personality for a cop. No bravado, and for the life of me, I haven't been able to wrench out a single war story from you."

"Finn, please stop," she murmured, feeling naked and exposed.

"But now it makes perfect sense. You're unassuming. No one would ever guess you're the Ghost. Quiet, observant, taking notes and names, calculating, always calculating." Finn's smile had turned to a grimace. "And then you had your break."

"Enough," Kirk said.

"What break?" Clinton asked.

"A psychotic episode, they called it. The Ghost killed a suspect, and with her bare hands."

"Because he murdered another undercover agent right in front of me." And because he was going to violate her, but she couldn't bring herself to tell anyone that part except Kirk.

Finn's eyes were full of hate now. "She strangled him. She needed him to keep her cover and blow that entire operation right off the map, but she listened to his last, gasping, dying breaths as she choked the life out of—"

"I said enough!" Kirk barked out. He jerked his chin toward Finn's cruiser. "Get the fuck out."

Finn cocked his head and glared at Kirk. "I miss the smog of the city. The noise. The people. The overcrowded sidewalks. It's too quiet out here, but a woman like Alison Holman can adapt to any environment to get what she wants." Finn turned and strode off for his cruiser. "Good luck figuring out her intentions, Shifter," he called. "No one can really know a ghost."

# FIFTEEN

Alison clenched her shaking hands at her side as Finn drove away. She was so angry she couldn't see straight, couldn't keep her breathing steady. She hated him for what he'd done. She'd been bonding with the shifters here, and now they would never trust her. Never accept her. She would be an outsider, just like the rest of her life.

Ghost. There was a fucking reason she didn't share her nickname.

She was tired of being invisible.

And now Harrison, Clinton, and Mason were looking at her with suspicion, and across the road, Bash and Emerson were scanning the others' faces, confusion pooling in their expressions.

Tears stung her eyes, and flames of embarrassment licked at her cheeks and ears.

182

"I don't have ulterior motives for being here," she rasped out as she stared at the ground. "I just like being around Kirk. I like being around all of you. I feel normal here." A tear streamed down her cheek and angrily, she dashed it away. "I was the Ghost because it was my job. I'm not undercover anymore." She drew in a deep, shaking breath. "I'm not anything."

Kirk hugged her tight against his side. "You feel like a lot to me."

"You're partner is an asshole," Bash called across the street. "I do *not* like him."

"I could kill him for you," Clinton said, a little too hopeful for comfort.

Kirk scrubbed his hands down his face and muttered, "Clinton, he might be an asshole, but it's still not polite to kill people."

Clinton stomped off, shoving his way roughly between Alison and Kirk. "I was just trying to help."

"Murder isn't helpful," Mason called.

Harrison blinked slowly, and his shoulders sagged like he hadn't slept in a year. "Alison, if you betray us in any way, there will be hell to pay."

"Hey, Harrison, you're a poet and you didn't even know it," Bash said as he approached. "Ally girl, you don't look like no ghost to me." Bash walked around her and poked her arm hard enough that it would probably leave a purple bruise in the morning. "You ain't even see-through."

"Just to be transparent," Kirk told Harrison. "Ally already told me about killing that drug dealer. It was self-defense."

"But she didn't tell you the other stuff," Harrison said, hands on his hips, head cocked, eyes dead. "I could tell by the look on your face."

"Those are my stories to tell," Ally said. "Eventually, I want to tell him everything, but no, Kirk doesn't know every detail about my life yet, like I don't know about every second of his. The nickname? It wasn't one I came up with, and I didn't like it. I want you all to call me Ally and look at me like I'm just another person. I'm trying my damndest to leave my past behind me. Kirk is my future. He's who I want to share stuff with, but before I came here, there was no one I trusted. I don't know who Finn talked to about my work, but that shit is classified. I was part of several operations that were covert and never discussed. He was out of line airing that information, but worse than that, he made you all look at me differently—like you'd never seen me before." She gestured toward the trail in the woods behind them. "The girl you saw at the falls. The one laughing and relaxing? That's the Ally I want to be. Not some stupid dead personality assigned to me because of the job I used to do. I want to feel"—she shrugged her shoulders up to her ears helplessly—"real."

A slow, proud grin washed over Kirk's face, and he murmured, "Truth."

And when she looked back at Harrison, he was smiling now, too. "Works for me. Come on Ghost Girl. Let's get drunk."

"Wait," she said stunned as the others walked away. "You're not going to rake me over the coals?"

"Nah," Mason said. "We can hear a lie. Finn didn't tell one, but neither did you."

She arced her shocked gaze to Kirk, but the smile had faded from his lips. His eyes were glued to her shoulder. "You're still bleeding," he murmured in a strange voice.

Sure enough, her puncture wounds were staining the T-shirt, which made perfect sense because it still hurt like hell. "Well, yeah. You bit me, Kirk. And then you jumped off a cliff with me."

His chest heaved as he lifted bright gold

eyes to hers. "I didn't realize humans were so fragile."

She frowned over her shoulder at the dark spots on the baggy shirt. "Well, I'm not dying."

Kirk shook his head and pulled her hand toward the biggest singlewide at the end of the trailer park. "I'm not taking care of you like I should."

"That's debatable." She lowered her voice and lightened her tone. "You did give me one awesomely explosive orgasm under the falls."

Kirk didn't seem amused, though. In fact, he didn't respond at all until they were up the porch stairs of a trailer with the lopsided numbers 1010 hanging beside the red door. "Why aren't you taking me to your trailer?"

"Because the walls are open, woman. It's a cesspool of mold spores, and I never gave a single thought to infection until just now. I took you swimming in a murky river with open wounds. I'm a fucking idiot."

"Not true at all, and you didn't bite me that deeply."

A long, low growl rattled Kirk's chest. "Stop lettin' me off the hook. Bash is convinced this place is magic."

"The trailer?"

"Yeah. Ten-ten has been to every trailer

park in Damon's mountains. It has been home to almost every single mate at one point, and they all swear the same, so call me superstitious, but it feels like a smart fuckin' idea to suck up some good vibes from this place." He pulled her inside and turned on her, then stood back a few paces.

She arched her eyebrows as he stared at her. "What am I supposed to do now?"

"Do you feel anything different? Do your wounds feel better?"

"Okay, you're being insane. Do you have a first aid kit in here? Oh, my God, there's a mouse!" She pointed to the rodent scampering across the floor. Nope, nope, hell nope, she didn't do mice. Alison bolted for the door, but Kirk was to her in a flash.

"It's Nards. Shhh. It's just Nards. He's a pet."

Was that her whimpering? Alison climbed up on the couch. "Why would you have a field mouse as a pet?"

"Well, because he's nice and gentle and...polite." Kirk frowned. "I thought it was weird at first, too, but now I have one of his babies in my trailer."

"On purpose?" Okay, she was screaming now.

"Yes. Her name is Teats, and she lets me hold her." Kirk cleared his throat and muttered, "She eats seeds from my hand."

"I had rats in all of my apartments in Chicago, and they were *not* nice. Not nice at all."

"Okay, well look." Kirk pulled a bag of jalapeño-flavored potato chips off the kitchen counter, knelt down, and handed one to Nards. And sure enough, the little mouse took it politely, then scurried off through the kitchen.

A shiver trembled up her spine, but she stepped gingerly off the couch and tried to regain her composure. Kirk stood slowly, and he looked like he was hiding a smile.

"What?" she asked.

"Nothing." Kirk cleared his throat and now his grin was stretching wider. "It's just you're this tough, badass, tatted-up undercover cop, and you're afraid of a pet mouse."

She smoothed her shirt farther down her knees and looked primly up at him. "Nards just surprised me is all."

"Nipples lives here, too."

"There are two of them?" Kirk hunched at the volume of her voice, so she lowered it to a less psychotic pitch and said, "That's just lovely."

"First aid kit is this way." He sauntered off through the kitchen.

"The way the mouse went?"

"Yep."

An open doorway swallowed him up, and now she was left in the middle of the living room alone, shifting her weight from side to side on the squishy laminate flooring and studying the small home. White walls, a sagging white ceiling with more than one leak stain, white kitchen cabinets, and green couches. There was an expensive looking television resting in the entertainment center, though, and the kitchen table looked high quality and handmade. Even the two dark wood ladder-back chairs beside the table looked fancy. She'd lived in way worse. As she ran her hands along the polished wooden countertops of the kitchen, she did get a strange chill up her spine, and this one wasn't from fear. It was from...she didn't know.

"You coming?" Kirk called from Mouseland.

Alison blew out a long, steadying breath and braved the bedroom, which, as it turned out, was huge and took up a third of the trailer. "Wow," she murmured. A thick cream and blue floral comforter was folded down invitingly on the bed, and flanked on either side was a pair of windows and old-fashioned hanging lights. There was a built-in dresser and two closet doors, and on the opposite wall was a bathroom. Kirk stood inside, ripping open a package of first aid supplies and muttering something too low for her to hear.

No Nards in sight, she leaned against the doorframe. "Are you okay?"

"Yeah, just worried. And my gorilla is ripping at my insides." He cast her a quick glance. "I didn't know it would be like this."

"Like what?"

"I'm rough, Ally. I mean, it's in my nature to be rough, and I didn't give two thoughts about how you would be affected by that." He laid out the supplies on the counter and lifted the hem of her shirt over her head, then peeled her damp tank top off as well. "Female gorilla shifters like being roughed up, with affection and in the bedroom, and silverbacks don't worry about them healing. I'm freaking out a little. I think I'm going to be shitty at this."

"It's okay, Kirk. You were raised around people like you. And then you were part of Kong's family group."

"But..." He waved his hand at her puncture

marks. At least they weren't bleeding anymore, but they did look angry and red. Kirk's head almost reached the ceiling in here, and his wide shoulders blocked an entire half of the wall from view. "I guess I didn't really give much thought to a human mate because I always assumed you would be different."

"A shifter, you mean?"

"Yeah."

She leaned her butt against the counter as he began cleaning her shoulder. "But you don't regret me, right?"

"No." Kirk shook his head and kissed her lips, just once. Just a single sip. "No, Ally, I have no regrets. I just have a lot to learn."

She smiled in relief, rocked forward, and rested her forehead against his bare chest. "So do I."

He chuckled deep in his throat, but swallowed the sound the instant she winced against the burn of the cleaner. "I hate this." He pressed his lips on top of her hair and let them linger there for a few moments before he started taking care of her again. "I hate seeing you hurt."

She ran a light touch over the gunshot scar on his shoulder. "I know the feeling."

As he bandaged her, his attention dipped

time and time again to her breasts and the tattoos that covered most of her left side, and she understood since she was drinking in his body as well. Muscular neck, perfectly defined pecs, eight-pack abs that flexed with every breath, and that light trail of hair that led from his belly button down into his jeans. With her fingernail, she traced the strip of muscle that delved over his hip bone and into the waist of his pants. And when she pulled his jeans forward and ran her touch along the edge of the fabric, a shiver took Kirk's shoulders, and he let off a soft groan.

"Woman, I just told you it's hard to be gentle. You're hurt. Don't push." His voice came out all inhuman and rough. Sexy silverback.

Feeling empowered that she could affect him so easily, she unsnapped the button of his jeans and gave him a naughty smile. "Should I stop then?"

His gaze on her hands, he shook his head with a jerk. Oh, beautiful man, with those blazing golden eyes and his chestnut hair falling forward against his sharp cheekbones. Alison pulled his zipper down slowly and unsheathed his thick erection. The head of his cock was swollen, and his length hard as stone, standing rigid against his belly. She ran her finger down his shaft and reveled in the satisfaction from his soft, needy growl.

"You're fucking killing me," he murmured as she slid down to her knees, taking his pants with her.

Kirk leaned back on the sink on one locked arm and ran his fingers through her hair with the other. Gently, she clamped her teeth on the head of his cock. He hissed, gripped her hair, and eased her back. He shook his head slowly, his hair twitching against his jaw with the motion. He looked feral right now. Inhuman. Wild. Hers. With a smile, Alison gripped his shaft and slid her mouth over him. His grip tightened in her hair, and he let off a soft sound deep in his throat, but he didn't pull her onto him. Instead, he let her set the pace, stroke after stroke, until his abs were twitching and his breath came ragged. And when his hips rolled with her motion, she knew she had him.

"Ally, Ally, Ally, stop. Stop or I'm gonna come in your mouth."

That sounded awesome, but Kirk eased out of her and blew three short breaths, then pulled her upward with a surprising amount of strength. She forgot how much of his power he hid. His chest was still making that sexy rumbling sound and, biting back an excited grin, she shimmied her damp shorts down her legs. Her insides were on fire, ready for him. Her body reacted to him like she was a firecracker and he was a match. His touch caused instantaneous, tingling, glorious heat.

He cupped her cheek, his expression intense the moment before his lips crashed onto hers. Swaying her from side to side, he turned her around until her back rested against his chest. He dragged kisses down her neck, one hand gently cupping her breast. His erection was hard against her back, and she was shocked at her reflection in the mirror. Cheeks flushed, lips parted and swollen, pupils dilated, nipples drawn up into tight little buds. A moment of mortification took her when he locked her arms against the counter top and she realized what he intended. If she didn't close her eyes quick, she was going to watch herself get banged by a Boarlander. She squeezed her eyes closed, but Kirk's deep, reverberating chuckle filled the small room.

"You should watch what you do to me, Ally."

"I've never done it in front of a mirror," she rushed out.

"Neither have I, but I want to see you. And I don't want to do this if I'm going to hurt your claiming mark."

Ooooh. There it was. And again, his gaze dipped to her bandages. He could've gotten away with four of those big square Band-Aids, but instead he'd wrapped up her entire shoulder like she was part mummy.

"I feel…" Kirk sighed and shook his head. "I'll Change if I hurt you."

"You're feeling protective."

Kirk nodded hard and lifted impossibly bright eyes to her. His gaze was so bright it was hard to hold in the mirror, and his face looked different now. Harder. Feral, as if his gorilla was right there ready to rip out of him.

Slowly, Allson spread her legs and arched her back, presenting for him as she watched his reflection. The corner of his lips turned up in a smile, and he dragged that hungry gaze of his down her back as he traced the outer edge of her tattoos with a light touch. "You're so beautiful."

Her throat tightened at how honest he sounded. He really did think her pretty. Strange, after feeling so unnoticeable for so long. He should hear how much he meant to her. Breath shaking, she whispered, "I've always felt invisible, but not with you."

"Not invisible, Ally Cat." He rested his chest against her back and kissed her uninjured shoulder with such tenderness, it made her want to cry. "You're all I see." In the mirror, his eyes were so open, so raw and vulnerable she wasn't alone in this freefall. Kirk was quieter, more reserved with his feelings, but he had jumped over the edge with her, just like on that cliff. He was in this.

She pushed backward, reveling in the feeling of his hard shaft against her. Kirk ran biting kisses down her neck, straightened his spine, then gripped her hips. She was so wet, so ready, and when he slipped the head of his cock into her, she moaned and rolled her eyes closed. He pushed into her deeply and grunted as his body went rigid, then relaxed as he pulled out slowly. When he rammed into her again, curiosity got the best of her. She opened her eyes. Behind her, Kirk was utterly sexy. Big, brawny man whose body had gone hard, and she wanted to watch his powerful thrusts into her. He was clenching his teeth, his eyes were glowing, and the growl in his chest was constant. And as beautiful as he looked right now, slamming into her, he also had an edge of panic in his eyes, his attention on her bandage.

He liked it from behind, and he liked it hard, but this wasn't going to work if his protective instincts were in overdrive.

She pulled herself forward and turned on him. He didn't fight her cutting them off so suddenly, just cupped her cheeks and kissed her lips. "I'm sorry," he murmured against them.

"Come here," she whispered, tugging his hand gently. Alison led him to the bedroom and pulled the comforter down.

"I'll hurt you," he said, balking.

"You won't." She climbed in and held up the covers. "We'll do this easy."

"Easy," he said in a voice that couldn't pass for human anymore. He slipped under the covers and pulled her close against his chest.

Alison slowed them down. She ran her hands over the mounds of his abs and then raked her nails gently up the strong planes of his back. Goosebumps rose under her touch, and he jerked his hips like he couldn't help himself. The growl in his throat settled and softened, and his dick throbbed against her belly. She'd worked herself up to white hot by touching him, so when he drew his fingertips up her hips, against the curve of her waist, over her ribs, then cupped her neck as he kissed her, she was nothing more than putty in his capable hands.

There he was—Gentle Kirk.

His focus was no longer on her claiming mark, but on pulling reactions from her body, and she loved this. Making love under the waterfall had been amazing, but this right here was perfect. It was saying "I love you" without words. It was him coveting her body and urging her closer to climax with just a touch of his hands. With kisses and nibbles. When he dragged his lips down the base of her throat and sucked gently on her breast, she gasped quietly and held his head, encouraging him to continue lapping at her sensitive skin as she rocked her hips against him. His movements were grace and power, and when he drew her nipple between his teeth and held her there, she was frozen with how good he felt against her right now. Slowly, he pulled her on top of him, held her close, his arms tight around her back as he rolled his waist and slid into her.

Kirk's heart was racing so fast she eased back and asked, "What's wrong?"

He was breathing too hard, eyes uncertain as he searched her face. Kirk brushed her hair behind her ear and shook his head like he was having trouble finding the words. He pushed into her again, easy, holding her gaze. "I've never...not like this."

Oh, she got what he was saying.

Kirk had fucked.

He'd never made love.

She kissed him to hide her happy grin. Nipping his lip, she murmured, "Good."

His kiss was so soft, so slow. He didn't force his tongue into her mouth or push their pace. Instead, he licked the closed seam of her lips, and when she parted for him, he slipped inside of her just enough for her to taste him. God, she loved him. They might not have said the words yet, but this right here was loving.

Kirk cupped her neck gently, his calloused hand on her skin as he angled his head and kissed her deeper. Allson set their pace slow because it seemed to be what he wanted now. And she wasn't in a rush. If she could stay in this moment forever with him, she would've, and from the careful attention he was paying her body with his touches, with his kisses, Kirk felt the same.

The pressure built fast—much faster than she'd expected at this pace. With every stroke he pressed into her, the tingling sensation deep in her belly increased until she had to close her eyes against the intense pleasure.

"No," he murmured, brushing the pad of his thumb across her cheek. "Look at me."

Feeling vulnerable wasn't so scary with Kirk. With a gasp on her lips, she rocked forward again and opened her eyes. She'd never seen adoration on a man's face before, but it was here in Kirk's gaze.

He gritted his teeth and blew out a breath, his body going hard as a rock every time he buried himself completely inside of her. "Ally," he gritted out.

"Me, too." Orgasm blasted through her, and she bowed against him, crying out his name.

He arched his neck back against the pillow and groaned as his cock throbbed inside of her. Heat shot into her over and over, matching her own release, but he never left the moment. Never closed his eyes, never let her go, never left her alone. He stayed there with her for every beautiful sensation. Every pounding aftershock.

And when he'd drawn every last one from her, he settled her onto the mattress beside him, pulled the comforter up to their shoulders and stared at her as if he couldn't believe she'd picked him. Cupping her neck, and brushing his thumb across her cheek, Kirk kissed her. Time passed with no meaning as he sipped at her lips, and she fell even harder. Nothing had ever felt like this—like another person was touching her soul.

"Ally?" Kirk asked.

She eased back and pushed his hair off his cheekbone so she could better see his darkening eyes. "Yeah?"

He swallowed hard and searched her face like she was the most beautiful thing he'd ever seen. "I see you."

And for the first time in a long time, she didn't feel like a ghost anymore.

# SIXTEEN

Kirk hesitated on Bash's front porch, hand lifted to knock against his newly painted red door. If he did this, it was the first step to breaking away from the Lowlanders.

Kong would fight to keep him.

But if he left now, he was saying goodbye to what he had up here in Boarland Mobile Park. He would have to move farther away from Ally, and leaving her alone and unprotected felt like more than his animal could handle. If he was completely honest with himself, his moodiness lately had been the direct result of thinking he would have to go back to Saratoga to continue his half-life.

Ally made him want more.

He needed to stop spiraling, and to do that, he had to make a decision and escape being stranded in the middle of two crews. Mason would likely leave the Boarlanders soon and go back to his life assisting Damon, but with every day that passed, Kirk felt more like this shitty old trailer park was home. It wasn't just Ally keeping him here either. Over the past week since they'd claimed each other, she'd cracked his heart wide open, and somewhere along the way, when he wasn't paying attention, the crew had snuck in there, too. Even fuckface Clinton.

Kirk ran his hand over his short beard, then rapped his knuckles loudly against the door.

Bash threw open the door, a big grin on his face. Kirk mirrored his smile. He couldn't help it. Bash's perpetual happiness was infectious.

"Hey, man," Kirk said.

"Second best friend." Bash wrapped him up in a back-cracking hug and clapped him on the shoulder blade hard enough to knock the wind from his lungs. The rough and tumble bear nearly killed with his affection, but with his mate, Emerson, Bash was gentle as a lamb. Kirk had always known he would be good at this mate thing.

"Emerson is in town with Audrey. You want a beer? Pizza rolls? I have a shit ton of boxed wine that my lady can't drink on

BOARLANDER SILVERBACK | T. S. JOYCE

account of the baby in her tummy." Bash grinned real big. "My baby." He was bragging, but Kirk let him. Bash had wanted a family for so long, and Kirk was damn happy for him.

Kirk lifted the envelope in his hand. "I actually wanted to have a meeting with you and Harrison. A business type meeting."

"Sounds like smart shit. Okay." Bash puffed out his chest and said in a formal voice, "Let's talk in my office."

Kirk snickered as he followed the giant shifter across the living room. They both ducked under the door frame of Bash's office, and he gestured to a futon covered in swirly, girly throw pillows. Emerson must've made this place her workspace for when she wrote pro shifter articles for the Saratoga Hometown News. Kirk huffed a private laugh at how much she'd come in and improved Bash's life. He had the nicest trailer in the park now, thanks to his urge to make a good home for Emerson.

Kirk sank into the thick cushion as Bash settled onto a rolling chair in front of his computer.

"So, you know I'm supposed to go back to the Lowlanders next week."

Bash's face fell, and his gaze dipped to

Kirk's work boots. "I don't like talking about that."

"Why not?" Kirk asked.

"Because it means you won't be here no more. You won't be here to yell at Clinton with me or see the fire pit we're building in a couple weeks. I won't hear your car rumblin' down the trailer park anymore, and you won't be here when Emerson has my cub. You won't be here for me."

Kirk swallowed a few times before he answered so Bash wouldn't see how affected he was. Finally he admitted, "I guess I wanted to talk to you before Harrison came over because I wanted to thank you."

Uncertainty slashed through the green of Bash's eyes. "For what? I didn't do nothin'."

"Untrue. You've done plenty, for this crew and for me. Remember when we were talking about you finding a mate, and you were scared you wouldn't be any good at it?"

"Yeah. I was wrong. I'm fuckin' awesome at it. Emerson says so all the time."

Kirk laughed and nodded his agreement. "Well, I remember when we were talking about that, I knew exactly how you felt. I understood your fear because I was afraid of the same thing—that I wouldn't be any good at being a mate."

"That's stupid," Bash scoffed. "You're a smart man, a hard worker, loyal as hell. You don't let people in easy, but when you do, you dig your heels in and make sure they're taken care of, no matter what. Ally is lucky, and you're lucky, too."

Kirk leaned forward, rested his elbows on his knees. "I don't know if I'll be good at this, but I'm trying. And I'll keep trying until Ally is happy, like you make Emerson happy. But part of that means sticking around."

"Sticking around?"

Kirk handed him the envelope, and with a frown marring Bash's jet-black brows, he opened it. He did a quick count of the twenty dollar bills inside. Bash's face went slack. "What is this, Kirk?"

"I heard you are the one to go to when we want to invest."

"You want me to grow your money?"

Kirk clasped his hands together and nodded.

"But I work for the Boarlanders. Kirk, I can take care of you, but not if you're getting paid by Kong down in Saratoga. I handle finances here, that's all."

"So if I stay here, you'll get me a 401k set

up?"

"Yeah." Bash smiled hopefully. "401k, investments, insurance, child education funds, whatever you want. I can make sure you retire on time with lots to live on. I can take care of you and Ally." Bash looked down at the envelope in his hands again and clutched it harder. "Stay. Not because of the money, but because it's where you belong. The other Boarlanders Clinton chased off? They weren't strong enough for this crew." Bash sighed. "I don't want it to feel broken around here again."

Harrison leaned against the office doorframe. "I second what Bash said. It won't be the same without you here. Look, I know you have a good job down in Saratoga and a nice setup near town. And I know it's hard on you finding your place in the pecking order here. But we were royally fucked at the beginning of the season, and you came in and helped us turn things around. We were limping along, and you propped us up. You and Mason both."

"What about your interviews?"

"Fuck the interviews, Kirk. You aren't replaceable, man. I was looking at hiring two loggers to put in the work you do. I don't like it, hiring new Boarlanders. I'd rather my crew choose to live here. Not for the money or the job stability, but because they fit here. You fit."

Kirk bit the side of his lip and ducked his gaze to his clasped hands because he'd never heard a better offer than that, nor a better combination of words. *You fit.*

"Kong won't want to let me go easy. It's not his fault. His animal has deep instincts and a small family group. He'll protect it."

Harrison inhaled deeply and shifted his weight, kicked the toe of his boot against a loose strip of flooring. "I suppose you're right. He'll require his pound of flesh." The alpha gave him a slow, steady smile. "Good thing I've been aching for a brawl."

"Nah," Kirk murmured. "This one is my fight."

# SEVENTEEN

Alison signed her name across another boring report that basically said nothing had happened for yet another day.

People weren't trying to hurt shifters here, and vice versa. With every day she spent at the post, she realized more that this job was utterly pointless. And apparently Finn felt the same because he was currently standing in front of her cabin throwing rocks at a tree trunk and muttering to himself.

Whatever. If he wasn't being such a mega-chode all the time, she would've cared about going out there and talking him through his pissed-off mood. But truth be told, he'd grown grumpier than Clinton with each passing day, and that was saying something.

This isn't what she'd imagined having a partner would be like. Undercover, she had to pretend not to know anyone who could be tied to the good side of the law, but when she'd been assigned Finn, she'd stupidly thought it would be like those cop shows on television. The die-hard bond where they would have each other's backs no matter what. In actuality though, if she was on fire, Finn wouldn't even bother to piss on her to put her out. Not after she'd thrown her support in for the shifters of Damon's mountains. He apparently thought her relationship with Kirk was some slight to him, but for the life of her, she couldn't figure out why. Her falling in love had nothing to do with Finn. Unless...

She stood and opened the door. "Do you have a crush on me?" she asked. It was better to ask direct questions to get a natural reaction.

Finn scrunched up his face and looked honestly disgusted. "Fuck no. You're too skinny, and you have too many tattoos. You probably have a thousand daddy issues, and I like long-haired brunettes with round asses." He squared his shoulders to her and hooked his hands on his hips. "Let me put it this way. I would only fuck you if I was blindfolded, so no, I don't have a crush on you."

She inhaled deeply, then blew out the

breath. She was pretty sure she hated him.

Finn went back to throwing rocks at the tree with more *oomph* this time.

The sun was setting behind Damon's mountains, and Alison was struck, as she was a hundred times a day, with the beauty of this place. At least it would've been beautiful if Finn wasn't muttering about her unattractive qualities loud enough to drown out the crickets and the birds.

An old, shiny black Jeep with fat tires and the top lowered blasted down the road from the mountains and skidded to a stop in the gravel right beside Finn, covering him in a cloud of chalky travel dust so thick he disappeared. Alison snorted as he launched into a cussing fit.

Audrey was behind the wheel, and Emerson was riding shotgun.

Harrison's mate shoved her sunglasses over her straight, dark hair and asked, "Do you want a girls' night with us?"

Emerson's strange gold-flecked eyes were bright with excitement as she leaned out the open window. "Say yes. Trust me. You want to go on this adventure."

"Where are we going?"

Audrey twitched a suspicious glare at Finn

and said in a careful tone, "Saratoga. Maybe leave that at home." She pointed a painted red nail at the badge clipped on Alison's jeans.

Okay, so maybe they were looking for trouble tonight.

"Kirk will be there," Emerson said, waggling her eyebrows.

"Great, then she should totally go and get gorilla-fucked in Saratoga," Finn griped.

"You sound like a jealous ex-boyfriend," Audrey said, her dark eyebrows arched high.

"Ha!" Alison laughed as she bolted for the cabin. "Give me two minutes." Inside, she unclipped her badge and set it on the bed. She was officially off-duty now and excited about the prospect of having some fun in Saratoga with Kirk and the Boarlanders. Plus, if she was honest, she was flattered as hell that Audrey and Emerson had invited her to hang out with them. They didn't have to do that, but over the last week, they'd all become friends. Those two were easy, non-judgmental, and they laughed all the time. It was good for her soul to be around people like them. She couldn't wait to escape the cloud of melancholy Finn cast over the post.

She peeled off her hoodie and changed into a fitted black T-shirt to cover her healing mark. She slathered on some lip gloss and smoked up her eyes in the mirror real quick, then bolted out the front door, feeling like a teenager sneaking out after curfew.

"Don't wait up, lover," she muttered through an empty smile as she jogged past Finn.

"Ooooh, Finn and Ally sitting in a tree," Emerson called out as Alison scrambled up the fat tire and into the back of the Jeep. "Kirk's gonna rip you in half for crushin' on his lady."

Audrey hit the gas and shouted over her shoulder, "Later Phlegm!"

He waved his hands to clear the dusty air and screamed, "It's Finn!"

Alison clutched her stomach and giggled as they blasted down the road toward Saratoga. In the front seat, Emerson was holding onto the top of the open frame, her wild curls whipping in the wind. "I don't know how you put up with him," she said over her shoulder.

"Girl, me either. I want to kick him in the sack ten times a day. He just told me he would only fuck me if he was blindfolded."

"Asshole," Audrey said with a disbelieving shake of her head. "Guess where we're going."

"Moosey's?"

"No, it's my day off!"

"Uhhh," Alison drawled. "I've only been to Saratoga to get groceries. I don't know what there is to do there."

"Your man has made a decision," Emerson called over the sound of the wind.

Alison gripped the two seats in front of her and pulled herself forward. "He's picked a crew?"

"Sure did."

Hurt, she relaxed against the back seat and watched the piney woods blurring by. "Why didn't he tell me?"

"Probably because he didn't want you to worry," Audrey said with a glance in the rearview mirror at her.

Sure, she wanted him to pick the Boarlanders for selfish reasons, but even if he picked the Lowlanders, she wouldn't be angry with him. "Why would I worry?"

"Because," Emerson said, twisting around in her seat. "To pledge to Harrison, Kirk has to fight his way out from under Kong."

\*\*\*\*

By the time they reached a giant barn that Audrey terrifyingly called the "fight house," it was full dark.

They parked in a field that doubled as a parking lot, then wove through rows of cars and knee-high grass until they reached a massive, dilapidated barn. Light shone from every crack between the wooden planks of the walls, and from inside came the sounds of rock music, cheering, booing, and whistling.

When Alison followed Audrey and Emerson through the open set of double doors, the noise level reached a deafening volume.

"I'm going to get us some beers," Audrey yelled by Alison's ear. She held up a couple of ten dollar bills and grinned. "I made a lot of tips today. Emerson, I'll see if they have water."

"Okay!" Alison and Emerson both said in unison, then giggled as Audrey disappeared into the crowed toward a hand-painted sign on the back wall that read *Booze*.

"Come on," Emerson yelled, tugging her hand toward the more concentrated crowd in front of them. "Audrey will find us. She's got those tiger senses. Let's see if we can get a good spot."

Around a fight ring—or what she assumed to be the fight ring because she couldn't see jack—there were wooden planks at different levels, and people were crowded onto them, yelling and waving fistfuls of cash. Finn would poop himself if he set foot in here. He'd probably give every single person a ticket and arrest as many as would fit in the back of his cruiser.

A sharp whistle sounded, and a tiny red-headed woman in a red plaid mini-skirt, black combat boots, and a T-shirt that read *Stick it in my wormhole* waved, then gestured them up onto one of the highest platforms. Alison grinned and waved back. She'd met Willa a couple times since she'd come to Saratoga. The fact she'd laced Finn's cookies with laxatives made her like the Gray Back Second even more. Alison helped Emerson scramble up a few platforms until they reached Willa.

"Hey, Tats! I thought you were going to miss it!" Willa called over the noise. "You're about to get super horny. There is nothing like seeing a shifter fight, and Judge has been working this crowd up all night for the grand finale. Lowlander Silverback versus Boarlander Silverback. This is going to be fucking epic!"

It was in this moment that Alison got her first look at the fighting ring in front of them. There was a row of bystanders in front of the platforms, but the old crates with standing room only were still pretty close. It was a make-shift ring with wooden railing. The floor inside was splattered with dark stains—blood. And circling the ring were two very familiar men.

"Is that Clinton and Mason?" she asked Emerson.

"Yep! They've been going at it for weeks up on the jobsite. I guess they decided to go all out here, bare-knuckle boxing. Probably best. Mason is a beast boar with long-ass tusks. Clinton's a brawler bear with teeth and claws, but Mason could have Clinton's innards on the ground before he knew what hit him."

As it was, Clinton and Mason were pounding the shit out of each other's faces, and their torsos were mottled purple and green from bruises in different stages of healing. Both their jeans were dotted with blood, and their massive torsos rippled with muscle every time they swung. This was a completely different side of the Boarlanders she'd ever witnessed.

"Beer!" Audrey called, scrambling upward from a lower platform. She held four red, plastic cups with the fingers of one hand, and a bottled water in her other hand, so Alison knelt down and helped her up by the arms until she was balanced on the platform with them. "Georgia!" Audrey called, passing a cup across Willa to the Gray Back park ranger with the golden curls.

Willa also got a beer, as well as Alison, and after a quick *clunk* of their cups in silent cheers, Emerson gulped at the water Audrey had brought right along with them. Mason's eyes were glowing like a demon now, and Clinton's looked almost white.

When a heavy-hitting song came on the loud speaker, Willa and Audrey booty-bumped Alison and danced to the beat. And as Alison looked down the platform to the other Gray Backs who were cheering on Mason, and then to a lower level where several of the Ashe Crew were screaming for Clinton, a wave of catching excitement blasted through her. She'd never had a group of friends like this. Being friends with her would've put someone in danger, but these people were tough. Resilient. Supernatural. They could handle the grit that came along with her life, and not only that, but they'd been completely accepting from the moment Kirk had declared she was his.

"Ally!" Harrison called from behind them. The Boarlander alpha looked grim, and his eyes were too light as he gestured her down.

"I'll be right back," Alison murmured to the

girls.

Harrison lifted her down and settled her on her feet, then reached up and took Audrey's hand, kissed it, and let his lips linger as a look passed between him and his mate that was so intimate, Alison's cheeks heated for witnessing it.

Harrison pressed his hand on Alison's back, guiding her toward a set of what looked like old horse stalls in the corner. "Clear a path," he growled at a rowdy group of onlookers. They parted immediately.

"What's wrong?" she asked when the masses thinned out.

"You'll see."

And the second she rounded one of the huge stalls, she did see. Kirk was pacing along the back like a caged animal, and nearly blocking the door with massively wide shoulders was a giant stranger who slid her a narrow-eyed look. His eyes blazed green, and there was a tattoo that stretched down from the sleeve of his T-shirt to his elbow. It was tribal with bold, dark lines of ink. Kong.

"Who are you?" the man asked in a gruff voice.

"She's mine," Kirk gritted out.

"What?" Kong asked.

"Baby," a pretty blond-haired woman said from against the wall. "If he wants out, you have to give him a way."

Kong shook his head over and over. The air was chokingly heavy in here. "He's in my group, Layla. It's not that simple." He jerked an angry gaze to Kirk. "You'll choose the Boarlanders over me? Tell me why. I thought you were happy in my family group, Kirk. If I thought you would cut out, I wouldn't have ever sent you up there in the first place."

"Kong," Harrison murmured.

"You shut the fuck up. He was supposed to help you, and I've been down at the sawmill limping along, waiting for him to come back to my crew. You left a fuckin' hole in my group, man. And what the fuck do you mean she's yours, Kirk?" Kong was yelling now. "You can't pick up your damn phone and let me know what's going on anymore?"

Kirk was growling a low, terrifying noise and pacing, always pacing, glowing gold eyes on Kong. He still had his shirt on, and a dark gray beanie covered his long hair.

"He has trouble saying how he feels," Alison murmured, neck exposed.

"But not with me!" Kong yelled.

Kirk was to him so fast he blurred, and he

slammed Kong against the wall with such force, it splintered behind the Lowlander silverback. "Fucking talk to her like that again, and I'll kill you."

"Kirk, be easy on him!" Layla pleaded. "I... Kirk, I'm pregnant."

"What?" Kirk asked, releasing Kong instantly.

"I'm pregnant." Layla's face crumpled, and her eyes filled with tears. "You were supposed to be in our group, helping us raise our child, but you want to leave. Can't you see? His animal can't just let you go."

"Tell me why," Kong rasped out.

Kirk ran his hand over his beanie, pulled it off, and chucked it at the wall. "Because, Kong! You and Layla will have a baby. Lots of babies if you're lucky, but I have no shot at a family if I stay under you. I'm not just some blackback in need of your protection. I'm a fucking silverback under a more dominant silverback. You stifle my instincts!" Kirk looked sick. "You always have."

A wiry man with dark, greasy hair popped his head into the stall. "You two are up next. Five minutes."

"Thanks, Judge." Harrison growled to Kirk, "I need to wrap your hands."

Alison didn't know what to do, but the air was so thick it felt like mud in her lungs, and she was going to suffocate soon. "I love him."

Kong and Kirk both jerked their gazes to her.

"What did you say?" Kong asked low.

Alison looked from him to Layla to Harrison to Kirk. Softly, she murmured, "I love you. And I think," she said, attention back on Kong, "he won't be able to love me back if you stifle his instincts again." Her voice dipped to a broken whisper. "And I really want him to love me back."

Kong stared at her for a loaded few moments, then sighed out the word, "Fuck." He kissed Layla's forehead, his hand resting gently on the slight swell of her stomach, and then he pulled his shirt over his head. To Kirk, he said, "I didn't know it was like that." He slid a reluctant glance to Harrison and nodded once. "Fight granted."

Shoulders shaking, Layla hugged Kirk's shoulders, and then followed Kong out of the stall.

Harrison's sigh tapered into a growl as he pulled Kirk's hand away from his side and began to wrap his knuckles with white tape. "Keep him still, will you?"

Alison looked behind her, but it was just her in here with them now, so she approached Kirk slow.

"What are you doing here?" he asked, his eyes on the work Harrison was doing on his hand.

"This is a big deal, Kirk. I should've heard about it from you."

"I have my reasons for not telling you."

"Because you are worried about me?"

"Yeah, Ally! Yeah. Ignoring that this place isn't all legal eagle and it could affect your *job*, you've gone through trauma, seen bloodshed. You told me yourself you were diagnosed with PTSD, and I don't want to make it worse on you. I want to protect you from this."

"Protect me from part of you? Because that's what this is, Kirk! It's a part of you that I wasn't invited to see. You have to fight. I get it."

"You don't."

"I do! You have a dominant animal side, and deep instincts I can't even fathom. I've already told you, I'm in this." She rested her forehead on his arm and murmured, "Hiding won't protect me, mate. It'll hurt me. You're choosing the Boarlanders, and we're in this together." She lifted her eyes to his. God, she hoped she had the words to make him understand. "You choosing a crew doesn't just affect you. You're choosing a crew for me, too."

Kirk clenched his jaw, and a muscle twitched there, but his voice lost the feral edge. "I didn't think about it like that."

"Other hand," Harrison demanded over the ripping sound of the tape.

"Yeah," she said, nodding. "Now go out there, win this fight, and make us Boarlanders."

He searched her eyes, his long, damp hair hanging in front of his face, his expression fierce, and his features sharp as glass. Kirk leaned down and kissed her hard. He nipped her bottom lip and released her, then rested his forehead on hers and murmured, "I will."

"All right, I've got to get his head on straight," Harrison said. "Bash is out by the rail. He'll make room for you."

She could feel Kirk's eyes on her as she walked out of the stall, and as she rounded the corner, she paused, took a steadying breath, chugged the beer in her cup, and made her way toward the ring. Did she want to see Kirk fight another dominant silverback? Hell no. But shifters lived by different rules, and she either had to accept all of him, or she had no business reaping the benefits of these friendships. She had to be strong enough to support him no matter the outcome of tonight.

Layla came out of a stall a couple down, wiping her eyes with the back of her hands, and that small gesture ripped Alison up on the inside. Maybe Layla wouldn't want comfort from the woman who was taking one of her family group, but she couldn't just stand here watching her sniffle and look heartbroken.

"Layla?" she asked.

Layla smiled slightly and shocked Alison to her core when she pulled her into a tight embrace. "It's okay. This is a good thing. Good for Kirk. He deserves happiness after everything he's gone through. Come on. We'll watch together, and afterward, everything will work out."

"Will it?" Right now, she felt like nothing was okay.

Layla gripped her shoulders and gave her an emotional smile. "It will. Kong and Kirk have work to do tonight, but they're the best men I've ever met. They'll be okay."

Layla took her hand and led her toward Bash, who, for the first time since she'd met him, wasn't smiling.

"What's wrong?" she asked him as they

finally made it to the front.

"Clinton and Mason hurt each other." His soft green eyes flicked to the corner where, sure enough, Mason and Clinton were both doubled over against the wall, surrounded by people preforming first aid.

"Do you want to go to them?"

"Can't. My bear won't let me leave you and Layla now, and besides, Harrison said wait here." His dark eyebrows arched high, and worry pooled in his eyes. "Ally, Kirk will get hurt tonight. He's my second best friend."

"He'll be okay, Bash Bear." Alison wished with all she had she felt as confident as she sounded.

The crowd was banging against the ring boards and stomping against the platforms in a steady rhythm that was gaining volume. The pace got faster as Judge stepped into the center of the ring. He held up his hands and spun in a slow circle, expertly quieting the onlookers. "Tonight, my friends, you're about to witness history. For the first time ever, two mature silverback shifters will go head-to-head in the ring." Judge gestured grandly to the opening at the corner of the ring. "You've seen him fight before. You know his brute strength, his deadly accuracy, his monster reach, and he's here tonight to defend his crew. The Kooooooooong!"

The crowd erupted as the dark-headed silverback strode into the ring, hitting the air, warming up his muscles. He clapped Judge on the back and lifted his hands into the air as he reached the center. He was a wall of solid muscle, and a smile twisted his lips but didn't reach his glowing green eyes.

"It's okay," Alison muttered to herself to settle her nerves. She gripped the wooden rails and blew out a sharp breath. All around them, bystanders were screaming at the top of their lungs, phones lifted, videotaping. Kong was a natural showman, revving up the crowd as he stood on the bottom slat of the wooden ring and cupping his hand behind his ear.

Layla looked sick beside her, and she knew the feeling. Alison shouldn't have chugged that beer.

"And the challenger tonight," Judge yelled over the noise. "One crew, two silverbacks, and this titan wants out. And there will be blood! Kirk Slater!"

The crowd went mad, shaking the wooden rails, stomping on the ground, screaming at the top of their lungs as Kirk sauntered into the ring, twitching his shoulders side-to-side with mellow air punches as he glared at Kong with pinpoint focus. He'd removed his shirt, and his body looked like a weapon. Massive shoulders that tapered to a V-shaped waist, abs tensed, the creases between each set of muscles deep. He flicked his damp hair to the side so the crowd could see his yellow-gold eyes. As he bounced from side to side, his muscle mass moved with the movement. His holey jeans sat low on his waist, and his arms were huge. Oh, she'd seen him without clothes, but he'd never had a reason to be tensed up and puffed out around her before. Here, in the blood-stained ring, slowly circling Kong, her mate looked like a terror-inducing, rip-roaring, badass beast.

Kirk slid his blazing gaze to her, then pointed to Bash. "You keep them out of the way."

Bash nodded jerkily and crowded Alison, and she had no doubt Bash could get her and Layla out of the way in a blur if he needed to.

"You know the rules, boys," Judge said, backing slowly out of the ring with an excited, gap-toothed grin. "There are no rules."

Kong and Kirk circled each other, tensed like cobras about to strike.

"Fight!" Judge yelled.

Oh shit, oh shit, oh shit.

Kong and Kirk charged each other immediately, each with their dominant arm reared back. When they connected with each other's jaws, a sickening thud rattled the air. There was a blur of hits too fast for her human eyes to comprehend, and she clutched Layla's hand when the woman beside her gasped.

Kirk was lethal, keeping up the pressure. Hit, hit, ribs, ribs, jaw. Kong was blocking, ducking, looked surprised by the pace Kirk was setting, but he adjusted, dodging a big hit and putting a shoulder in Kirk's middle, tackling him to the ground. They slid across the ring, and Kong reared back, one hand around Kirk's throat as he pulled the other fist back to blast it into Kirk's face. As he dropped the hammer, Kirk shoved Kong's wrist and jerked his face out of the way just in time, and Kōng's fist splintered the wood right next to Kirk's cheek. He bucked and swung his way out from under the Lowlander, but they were fighting too close now, and Bash yelled at the crowd behind them to, "Back up!"

Kirk's gold eyes flashed as he was thrown toward the railing in front of Alison, and at the last second, he fell to his hands and feet, skidding to try and avoid them. Bash hugged her and Layla up tight and grunted as something solid hit him in the back.

A series of pops sounded, and Alison's blood curdled as she heard a room-shaking roar. "Aw, fuck," Harrison said beside them. "Kirk!"

Alison stared in horror as she caught a glimpse of Kirk's gorilla, battle ready, canines exposed as he paced the ring right in front of them. She knew what he was doing. Kong had lost his head, lost his bearings, but Kirk had done what he could to stop the fight from hurting her.

All around her, the crowd was screaming a deafening sound. Countless phones were pointed at where her mate was pulling himself along on powerful arms and legs. He was pitch black, his blazing golden eyes glued to Kong.

Kong had crashed against the ring on the other side, snapping several boards in half. He stood to his full, imposing height slowly. There was a gash under his eye, and red was streaming down his cheek, but he didn't favor it as the feral smile transformed his face to something terrifying. He inhaled deeply and yelled, the veins in his neck bulging as his teeth elongated. The sound of his voice turned to a roar as his gorilla exploded from him.

"Oh, my God," Layla said in a horrified whisper. "Harrison, do something!"

The Boarlander alpha shook his head, his eyes horrified. "You and I both know there's nothing I can do to stop this now."

"Shit. Get back!" Alison screamed, waving her arms to the crowd.

There wasn't time. Both silverbacks stood on their hind legs, beat their chests with a drumming sound that echoed pure power through the barn, and then they charged. The clash of their massive bodies sent a wave of energy through the air that knocked Alison backward. She staggered on her feet as Bash held her and Layla in place. The *thud, thud* of the fighting gorillas pounding their fists against each other's skin sounded time and time again, and now there was blood. A flash of teeth told her why, and when the fight tumbled toward them again, Kirk bailed, launching himself onto a steel post behind her and Layla.

"This is insane!" the guy next to Layla yelled through an excited grin. He arced his cell phone with Kong's movement as the silverback launched out of the ring and after Kirk. They climbed up to the rafters of the barn, and Kirk swung around, one arm gripping the wood above him, the other out to catch Kong's full force as he barreled into him. With a blur of violent motion, the silverbacks plummeted to the floor and landed hard in the ring. Alison screamed and clamped her hand over her mouth as the flooring underneath her feet shook like an earthquake.

She couldn't tell who was winning. Couldn't tell them apart as they pummeled each other, a flash of teeth and jet-black fur. Someone was painting the ring in crimson. Who was it? Kong? Kirk?

Beside her, Layla shook her head and buried her face against Alison's shoulder. Alison cupped Layla's face and murmured, "It'll be okay. They're fine. It'll be over soon." Maybe she was telling the truth, she didn't know. Right now, it felt like this was stretching on for eternity.

One of the gorillas was thrown against the floor, and with a flash of gold eyes, the dominant silverback slammed his fists on either side of the other's face.

The gorilla's stopped fighting, chests heaving as they glared at each other. The crowd quieted as something wordless passed between the brawling beasts.

Kirk lifted his chin, then slowly backed off

Kong. And when Kong stood, he didn't charge again like Alison feared. Instead, he tilted his head, exposing his neck to Kirk.

"It's done. It's done," she chanted to Layla in a shaking voice.

Kirk gave a slow, bored blink like he hadn't just been in a bloody battle, then strode with slow, deliberate steps toward her. Alison froze when he lifted the back of his smooth knuckle to her cheek. His face morphed to a frown as he stared at the drop of moisture there. Afraid she would lose it in front of everyone, Alison grabbed his hand, kissed his knuckles.

And suddenly, Judge was announcing Kirk as the winner, and Bash was lifting Alison over the rail like she weighed nothing at all. Dragging a steadying breath into her lungs, Alison walked beside Kirk as he left the ring, and they were followed closely by Kong and Layla as the crowd went wild and surged toward them.

Everything came in flashes after that.

The fur on Kirk's shoulder was matted and dripping.

The Ashe Crew and Gray Backs were trying to keep the crowds at bay.

So much yelling.

Cell phone cameras everywhere.

Audrey told her, "Everything is fine." Was everything fine? She'd never seen a shifter battle on television or the Internet. Especially not while they were in animal form. Alison felt numb.

She stumbled beside Kirk, and he gripped her arm in his massive hand, his eyes concerned. He was worried about her tripping over her own shoes? He'd just gone to war with King Fuckin' Kong.

Judge handed her money. He was so happy. Alison stared dumbly down at the wad of cash in her palm. "I don't want this."

"It's for Kirk. He earned it."

"Back off, Judge." Clinton was there, bloody and bruised. One of his eyes was swollen shut, and he was only talking out of one side of his mouth. "She said she don't want it."

With a shake of her head, Alison handed the money to Clinton and wiped her palm on her jeans as if that would remove the grimy feeling of the twenty dollar bills.

Harrison's eyes were hard as he shoved a man who got too close to Audrey for a picture of the gorillas.

Clinton was yelling. So was Mason, and now Emerson was with them, and Bash was protecting his mate's stomach as they made their way toward the exit.

So much jostling. Kirk wrapped his massive arm around her back and moved her in front of him, then curled his lips back at the solid wall of onlookers fighting for a closer look and screaming questions at them. She looked back at Layla who was pale in the dim lighting, eyes worried. Beside her, Kong was bleeding. A lot.

Matt from the Gray Backs appeared through the crowd, a first aid kit thrown over his shoulder. Had he stolen it? Such a huge, pristine kit didn't make sense here in the dirty barn. Chills textured her arms, and Alison rubbed them to try and rid herself of the tingling sensation. Was she in shock? How weak. She'd only been a witness to the battle.

No, that didn't seem right. She'd felt right there with him, affected blow by blow, hurting alongside her mate.

"It's the bond," Layla said from behind, as if she could read her thoughts.

Oh. The bond. More she didn't know about.

Outside, Kirk cast her a lingering glance over his shoulder, then took off, charging away from the crowd, Kong following directly after him. They disappeared into the woods behind the field where all the cars were parked.

"They have to shake the crowd," Harrison explained to Alison as he drew Audrey close to his side. "Don't worry. We'll find them."

# EIGHTEEN

It took half an hour bouncing around in the back of the Jeep on old dirt roads to track down Kirk.

And by the time Audrey pulled them into a clearing that looked like it was a local hangout for muddin', Kirk and Kong were Changed back to their human forms and dressing in a couple pair of jeans Matt pulled from a duffle bag, while Willa stood off to the side, eyes a blazing green color Alison had never seen on her. Apparently the boys had riled up her inner bear, and from what Alison had gathered, Willa's animal was a dominant she-grizzly.

Willa was funny as hell, but Alison made a mental note not to piss her off in the future. Really, after seeing the brutal power with which Kirk and Kong had fought tonight, she was disinclined to piss off any shifter.

The headlights illuminated the silverback shifters who were talking low to each other. Matt was administering first aid to the side of Kong's neck, but it was Kirk who kept drawing Alison's attention.

His eyes were still too bright to be human, and the wisps of conversation carried on the wind made his voice sound like a snarly demon's, but it was his body that drew the gasp from her lips. Harrison and Bash were trying to get the bleeding stopped on his shoulder, and his entire torso was black and green with bruising.

"Oh, my gosh," Emerson murmured from the front seat.

Alison scrambled down from Audrey's jeep on shaking legs, then ran across the knee-high grass that stood between her and her mate. Kirk's gaze, reflecting like an animal's in the headlights, collided with hers, and he broke away from Bash and Harrison. He was favoring his arm to his ribs, but he strode toward her at a quick clip, his good arm out.

She meant to go in easy so she wouldn't hurt him, but Kirk pulled her against him hard and rocked them slowly back and forth, his cheek pressed against her hairline. His chest was heaving, and his heart pounded like a drum. He smelled like iron, but he was here. He was whole, alive. Okay.

"I'm sorry," he murmured.

She laughed in surprised disbelief and eased back. "You're sorry? Why on earth would you be apologizing to me right now? You did nothing wrong."

"Disagree," Harrison barked, eyes narrowed on his glowing phone. "And now excuse me while I get my ass chewed out." He accepted the call and said, "Hey Cora. Before you give me what for, you should know I couldn't stop it." Harrison cocked his head and winced, pulled the phone away from his ear as if Cora Keller was yelling. "Well, you can blame Kirk and Kong for any bad press. Tell me something. Would you send Boone in there to break up two warring silverbacks?" He paused. "Didn't think so. I wanted to survive. Yeah." Harrison sighed, rubbed the heel of his hand against his eye as if he was getting a headache. "Yeah. Will do, just give me a call tomorrow and tell me what I can do to clean this up."

Kirk lowered his lips to her ear and whispered, "I'm sorry you had to see that. I couldn't stop the Change. My animal didn't like

239

feeling so out of control when you were that close to the fight. Next time you'll have to watch from the platforms."

"Next time?"

Kirk pressed his lips against her forehead. "Kong and I are settled, but like I told you—"

"You'll have to fight. Because of me."

When he finished his kiss with a soft smack, he leaned back. He had a sexy, crooked smile. "You're worth it."

She sighed and shook her head as she studied his torso.

"Hey," he murmured, hooking his finger under her chin and lifting her gaze to his. "I'm okay. We're okay." Another breathtaking smile. "I got us a crew."

"Boarlander Crew!" Beck called

"Boarlander Crew!" Audrey and Emerson said in unison.

Clinton and Mason stood off to the side, but they both murmured, "Boarlander Crew."

And now Harrison's scowl lifted in a slow smile as he approached. He clapped Kirk on the good shoulder. "Welcome to my crew."

"We fit," Kirk said.

Alison didn't understand what he meant, but Harrison grabbed him by the back of the head and pressed his forehead to Kirk's. And for a loaded second, the two behemoth men stayed just like that, sharing air, and then Harrison slapped him roughly on the back again and said, "Damn straight, Slater. You and Ally fit. Boarlander Crew."

Alison blinked back the burning in her eyes as it dawned on her what had just happened. They were pledged now. Audrey pulled her away from Kirk and into a hug, and Emerson wrapped her arms around both of them.

Kong began a slow clap, and Layla joined him. Willa whistled, and Matt stood from where he was packing away first-aid supplies. Some of the Ashe Crew was standing off in the shadows, and they clapped, too. As Alison was passed around for hugs and congrats, it became harder and harder not to cry as the potency of this moment slid over her shoulders.

She had a place now.

She had people.

Her mate watched her with a proud smile as his body shook from handshakes and back claps.

She had Kirk.

And when Layla pulled her in tight, Alison lifted her gaze to the twinkling stars above them and squeezed her back.

"Take good care of him," Layla murmured.

"I promise I will."

"You two come by Sammy's this weekend, and we'll celebrate it up right. Drinks will be on me."

"Thank you," Alison rasped out past her tightening vocal cords.

And when she let go, her gaze drifted to Kong, who stood tall under a towering spruce. He didn't look angry or hurt like she'd expected. He looked...relieved.

She approached slow, and after a moment of hesitation, she hugged his waist gently. "I'm sorry for your loss."

Kong chuckled a deep, reverberating sound and hugged her back. "No loss. I have a baby on the way with the mate I always dreamed of. Kirk deserves the same. If you need anything, you call us. Just because you two aren't Lowlanders doesn't mean we won't be there for you."

Unable to speak, Alison nodded and released him.

She made to leave, but he said, "Ally?"

God, she loved the sound of her nickname on her friends' lips. She had *friends* now. The real kind, not the pretend ones she'd made as

Ghost.

"Yeah?" she asked, turning.

"What you said in that stall. Telling Kirk you love him in front of everyone?" Kong pursed his lips and nodded. "That means a lot to men like me and Kirk. I'm really glad he picked you."

She arched her attention to Kirk, who was talking low to Bash as the bear shifter poured a bottle of water over his injured shoulder. He must've been in pain, but when he caught her staring at him, Kirk gave her one of those smiles that made everything seem right in the world.

"I'm glad he picked me, too."

****

Kirk changed gears and hit the gas on a straightaway, then immediately slid his hand over her thigh again. It was the middle of the night, and she should've been exhausted, but the adrenaline dump from earlier had done something strange to her. She hadn't crashed. Instead, she felt jittery.

Kirk cast a slight frown at her leg as she shook it in quick succession. His eyes were still too light, and there was a soft rumble in his chest that hadn't diminished since they'd left the woods. She suspected his animal was riled up due to pain. She'd watched Bash put his dislocated shoulder back into the socket, and though Kirk rarely showed his hurt, he'd winced hard and grunted under Bash's none-to-gentle touch.

At least his bruises were healing. Matt had told her Kirk had a few cracked ribs, but already, they seemed to be healed. He wasn't favoring them or his shoulder anymore. Shifter healing was miraculous.

Kirk's gaze drifted from the road passing under his headlights to her shaking leg again. He squeezed her thigh gently. "Ally, tell me what's wrong so I can fix it."

Deliberately, she stilled. "Sorry. I'm still a little worked up from tonight. I've seen a lot, but that was insane." The memory of Kong and Kirk beating their chests as they charged each other flashed across her mind. "You hide a very powerful animal from the world."

Kirk snorted. "Not anymore. Kong and I are probably all over the Internet right now. Cora is gonna skin us alive." He slipped a finger into the ripped hole on the thigh of her jeans, and unintentionally, she rocked her hips.

A wicked smile curved Kirk's lips. "You worked up, too?"

"I don't know what you mean," she lied.

"Fighting does that to me." He drew her hand against his crotch, and she gasped at how rigid his erection was. "I wanted to take you into the woods and fuck you hard when you showed up. Part of it is instinct. I get possessive and desperate to touch you. And part of it is that tight shirt you're wearin' tonight. You look damn good in black, your tats showing down your arm, that sexy as fuck hair, that smoky eye shit you're wearing that makes your eyes look brighter blue. Tight shirt showing off those perfect tits, and those tight jeans hugging your perfect ass. It's hard to focus around you."

"Is that why Harrison kicked me out of the stall? To get your head on straight?"

"Probably."

Teasingly, she gripped his erection over his jeans and dragged her hand up the length of him. "Only half an hour and we'll be home."

Kirk lifted his hips slightly, chasing her touch, and shifted gears to maneuver the winding mountain road. The roar of his Mustang overpowered the rap music on the radio as he shifted again and gunned it on a straightaway. "Too long."

"I should stop so you don't drive us off a

cliff," she murmured. She moved to pull away, but he grabbed her hand and pressed it on his dick again, then rolled against her palm with a soft, huffed breath.

Kirk's hair was flipped over to the opposite side of his face, giving her access to drink in all of him, from his glowing eyes to the slight frown of intensity that furrowed his dark eyebrows. Thick neck, defined pecs, and his arm flexed as he gripped the wheel tighter. His abs were perfect mounds of muscle, rippling as he pushed against her hand again. Big, powerful legs pressed against his hole-riddled blue jeans and damn, Kirk was the sexiest man she'd ever laid eyes on.

Alison unfastened his jeans and pushed them down far enough to release his rigid shaft with its swollen head and silky skin. As she drew a light touch up his long, thick length, his dick throbbed, and a drop of creamy moisture appeared on the tip. She loved how ready he was for her all the time. How affected he was by her touch and by the way she looked. Sexual heat like this hadn't existed before he'd come into her life.

If she was unsure of what he wanted before, that question was laid to rest the second he wrapped his fingers gently in the back of her hair and pulled her face toward his lap. Good mate, telling her what he wanted. With a private smile, she gripped him and slid her lips over his cock. He tensed under her and let off the sexiest groan, deep in his throat. Alison eased off, then took him in her mouth again. His fingers tightened in her hair, but he didn't push. She could taste his delicious saltiness and reveled in the fact she could draw this reaction out of a man like Kirk. Powerful, masculine, growly gorilla shifter, and he wasn't even complaining at the slow pace she set with her mouth.

His body tensed and relaxed with each stroke of her lips and tongue, and now the car was slowing. Downshift, hard right turn, and the road turned uneven.

She was so wet now, so revved up because of those sexy noises her mate was making over the blare of the radio. When Alison slid her hand down her belly and into the front of her jeans, Kirk slammed on the brakes, skidding to a stop. He threw it into park and leaned his seat back, then pulled her onto his lap until she straddled him.

"Want to see you touch yourself," he said in a gravelly voice, his glowing gold eyes riveted between her legs.

Alison arched her back as he unzipped the front of her jeans. With a soft gasp, she slid her hand into her panties and pushed her finger inside of her. She rolled her hips, barely touching Kirk's dick with the movement.

He gripped her thighs hard and spread his knees wider.

She let off a soft moan, grabbed the back of his neck with her free hand, and pushed her finger into herself again.

The growl in Kirk's throat was constant now. So sexy. Feral. *My mate.*

The door opened, and Kirk had them out of his car in an instant. It was all she could do to hold onto him as he rushed them out onto a dirt road in front of his car. The radio was still blaring, and the headlights lit up the woods around them. Kirk laid her down on her back and stripped her jeans off, his movements jerky and desperate. He tucked the loose fabric under her butt, and she spread her legs wide for him, feeling drunk on his touch.

He lifted slightly on his knees and slid his thick shaft into her. As he eased out, he rolled his eyes closed and gritted out a relieved sound.

Alison raked her nails down his chest as he locked his arms on either side of her head.

Every muscle of his beautiful body was flexed and cast in soft shadows while the headlights illuminated his striking, powerful shoulders over her.

Kirk shoved her shirt upward and lowered himself onto her belly, kissed her hard, rammed his tongue into her mouth as he pushed into her again, stretching her with his girth. His hard body felt amazing against her as he moved in smooth, commanding thrusts.

Alison was gone. Each of her breaths brought a needy sound that got louder with every stroke into her, and the volume of the growl in Kirk's throat matched until he threw his head back, yelled out as he slammed into her harder.

The light of his car was blinding now, and the stars above were too bright to look at. Closing her eyes tightly, she bowed against the earth, meeting him blow for blow until the first drum of her orgasm shattered her. Her release intensified, and she screamed out his name.

With a feral-sounding growl, Kirk pulled out of her and took himself in hand. He gripped his dick and lifted above her. She couldn't take her eyes away from his graceful movement as he pulled stroke after stroke.

Her orgasm pulsed on between her legs. He was letting her watch! Kirk locked an arm near her cheek and leaned forward. And as his stomach tightened, the first warm shot of his release splashed onto her belly, followed by another and another. His hips jerked, his eyes locked on hers. As he emptied himself completely, he ground out, "Mine."

Oh, there was her wild man. Her wild mate. There was the possessive shifter side that sat just under the surface, marking his territory. She was his. Maybe she had been from the moment they'd seen each other.

She traced the bite mark she'd made on his shoulder. Lifting off the ground, she kissed the scar gently, then lay back and touched the dark scruff that shaded his jaw. As he pressed his lips against her palm, she whispered, "Always."

# NINETEEN

*Always.* Kirk put his car into park and let his hand slip from the steering wheel. The way she'd said "always" when they'd been together in the woods had split his heart open so wide it was almost painful.

Ally inhaled deeply, but didn't wake up in the dim street light that illuminated the yard of her cabin. The soft glow lit up her cheek and, carefully, Kirk brushed her short blond hair from her face. It felt like silk and had soft waves to it. Her roots were darker to match her lashes that rested against her cheeks. A natural brunette, but he liked her like this. She'd been affected by her years undercover and looked accordingly tough, but he was the one she shared her real self with. Beautiful mate.

He relaxed against the headrest, just

staring at her because he could. Usually, she grew self-conscious under his prolonged attention, likely a product of her phantom past. Invisibility had meant survival, but she was safe here with him. He would make sure of it. He would make sure she knew she was protected, and he would be the lucky one who got to watch her open up.

God, she had him. Ally didn't even realize how much he cared about her. How devoted he was. How much she owned him, body and soul.

His decision to choose the Boarlanders wasn't just about him. Sure, he'd grown an undeniable loyalty to Harrison and his crew, but choosing them also meant another layer of safety for his mate. She had an undercover past, and he didn't know how many enemies she'd found in that life, but he knew the crews of Damon's mountains would go to war for their own. Winning his freedom from Kong tonight meant Ally was now a part of this place.

Kirk searched the dusty gravel parking lot in front of her cabin. The road blocks were up, but he would drive around them like he always did. He'd been so damned tempted to bring Ally back to Boarland Mobile Park, to

1010, just so he could sleep beside her all night. He'd never done that with a woman before. In fact, Ally was taking more of his firsts than she knew. Being with her felt different from every other relationship in his life. She was more.

She was richness and fulfillment. She was polish on a dirty penny, and now he felt like his entire life had led him here, to this life with her. Fuck where he came from. Fuck his messed up people and the treachery Fiona had pulled. Fuck every single thing except for the life he was building with Ally.

She deserved everything. To be provided for, to feel safe. She deserved his fealty and the protection of his body. She deserved to be happy, and he was going to work his ass off every day for the rest of his life to give that to her if she would let him.

He had to be up in a few hours for one of the last long days of logging season so he couldn't afford to stall anymore. Being exhausted on the jobsite put his crew at risk. *His crew.*

Kirk huffed a soft chuckle. Damn, it felt good to belong to something bigger than himself. To something that didn't stifle him or leave him hungry for a life he could only imagine.

Ally had done that—made him choose a future.

Kirk got out of his Mustang, shut the door easy, then strode around the front. Ally sighed the cutest little sleep sound he'd ever heard as he unbuckled her and lifted her from the car. She wrapped her arms around his neck and nuzzled her cheek against the base of his throat and now his gorilla was practically clapping inside of him like a giddy teenager. She never looked at him like he was a monster, and she didn't mind his rough edges like he'd been afraid of. Instead, the more he exposed of himself, the better they seemed to fit together.

It felt so damned good to have found his person. His partner. His mate. His Ally.

He maneuvered her front door open. As the swinging screen door creaked closed behind him, he strode through the office area to her bedroom. Settling her gently on the mattress, he lowered to his knees beside the bed and gave into his urge to touch her. Kirk drew her to the edge and hugged her securely against him. Inhaling deeply, he committed her scent to memory. Shampoo, soap, earth, Ally...him. He liked best the way she smelled right after they'd had sex, and screw whatever monstrous things that said about him.

"Ally," he murmured.

Her eyes fluttered open, and she stretched against him like a sleepy feline.

"Earlier you said something to me, and it took me by surprise. I didn't respond like I should've. You were brave enough to tell me you loved me, and I didn't tell you how I felt about you."

"Then tell me now, you big sappy monkey," she whispered.

The words caught in his throat. Not because he didn't feel them with every fiber of his being, but because he'd never said them before to anyone. He buried his face against her neck. "I love you."

Her cheek swelled with a smile against his. "Now say it while you're looking at me."

He sighed and eased back, searched her eyes in the dim streetlamp lighting that filtered through her bedroom window. "Ally Cat Ghost Holman—"

"Stop it and be serious."

"I love you."

The smile dipped from her face, then returned slowly, like she couldn't believe he was saying these sentiments to her.

"You had to have known how I felt, Ally."

"Yeah," she whispered. "But it's different hearing you say it out loud. Feels better than just hoping you feel the same as I do."

Kirk kissed her soft lips, then stood to leave, but she held his hand. "Don't go. Not yet. Can you just stay here with me for a little while? I don't want the night to end. Not yet."

"Okay." Kirk kicked out of his shoes and climbed onto the bed behind her, spooned her against his chest, and nuzzled his face into the back of her neck.

And then Ally—his Ally—took another first from him as he fell asleep beside her.

**** 

Kirk's warmth left her back, and Ally pouted sleepily. She was still lying on top of the covers, and the only thing that had kept her from the chill in the air was her big, naturally hot-natured mate.

But when she turned around to beg him to lie back down beside her, the look on Kirk's face had her sitting straight up beside him. He had his head canted, his ear directed at the window to the back yard. Outside, gray dawn light streaked through the sky, which made it easy to see the suspicion on Kirk's face.

"Can you hear that?" he asked.

She listened really hard. Other than a few

morning birds chirping outside and her own breathing, she didn't hear anything. "No. What does it sound like?"

He narrowed his eyes as if searching for the right words. "Like something tiny and high pitched. Like the whine of a mosquito, but it's constant. A buzzing. Electric maybe. It's almost too high for me to hear but I had trouble sleeping because it doesn't belong out here."

She ran her hands over the gooseflesh on his back. Something had his instincts up.

"Do you have a computer?" he asked low.

"Yeah, in the other room. It's turned off, though."

"Huh." He was doing it again, angling his ear toward the window. In a distracted voice, he said, "I'll be right back." Lithely, Kirk slid out of bed and padded silently out of the room.

In a less graceful maneuver, Alison flopped out of bed like a tuna fish and bolted for the peg on the wall where her holster was hung. She pulled her Glock and checked the clip, then slipped out the back door behind Kirk.

He was standing in the clearing, hands on his hips as he scanned the canopy above. He slid one bright-eyed glance at her over his shoulder before he strode up to a giant pine and climbed up the branches so easily she lowered her weapon to her side and gawked. Midway up, Kirk gripped the trunk and yanked something off the bark. Then just as gracefully and swiftly, he climbed back down and stared at something small and black on the palm of his hand.

Ice prickled her blood as Alison approached him slowly, gun angled toward the ground, eyes glued on the contraption. "What is that?"

He rolled his palm, turning the device over in his hand, and she gasped as she recognized the lens of a small camera. She'd used similar ones in her years undercover.

Kirk lifted his troubled gaze to hers. "You're being watched."

# TWENTY

Alison leaned against the doorframe to her bedroom and studied Finn as he reclined in the office chair and tossed a tennis ball into the air. He looked calm-as-you-like, but her red flags had been flashing non-stop about him lately.

He'd become combative and hard to hold a conversation with. After the influx of videos from the silverback fight, he'd spewed his disdain for Kirk and her involvement with him. Thank goodness her years undercover had made her hard to track, because so far, no one had listed her name yet in the videos of the fight. She'd been there, followed by the cell phone cameras as she'd walked beside Kirk out of that barn. On the outside, she'd looked calm and collected, head held high, her hand on Kirk's ribs as Kong and Layla had followed

259

them directly, the other shifters of Damon's mountains pushing back the crowd around her. If anyone had questions about Kirk being paired up before, those had been put to rest with the #kirksqueen that was circulating the Internet.

Finn had gone bat-shit crazy over the footage—yelling, calling superiors, and filing formal complaints, but the cold, hard fact was that her relationship with Kirk wasn't illegal. Marriage and claiming marks were, but she hadn't told anyone she bore his scar, so she was free to date him all she liked. At least for now, until the government tried to strip the next round of rights from shifters.

So far, the footage hadn't damaged public perception of shifters that Cora could tell. In fact, she'd told Harrison the silverback battle had boosted curiosity on shifter culture, and her pro-shifter website had been surging with hits and questions. Harrison's relief had been almost tangible. They hadn't taken a giant step back in public relations and now, at the Boarland Mobile Park, Alison was utterly happy. But here at the post, Finn worked very hard to drain her.

For the last two days, she'd kept the fact that Kirk found the cameras a secret, waiting for some kind of reaction from Finn, but so far, he showed no signs of suspicion. Her mind had immediately gone to her partner when Kong had tracked down five cameras, all pointed at her house, while the woods behind Finn's house boasted none.

Alison opened her palm and glared at the small black device she'd disabled. Someone had been watching her, but maybe Finn didn't know about them. She hoped he didn't. That betrayal would sting like a lash if he did. He was an anti-shifter jerk, but he was also her partner who was supposed to have her back.

"Finn?"

"No."

She'd expected that clipped response. It was his go-to whenever she tried to talk to him. Alison screwed her face up with concern and pitched her voice higher. "Look what I found in the woods."

He dropped the tennis ball and turned in his chair, his eyes flashing with worry. And for an instant, when he locked eyes on the device on her palm, there was a spark of recognition. Mother fucker.

"Where did you find that?"

"In a tree. Finn, someone is watching us. Why do you think they would do that? *Who* would do that?"

His bright blue eyes tightened at the corners, and he stood and retrieved his ball. "Hell if I know, Holman." Now he wasn't meeting her gaze, and she had to hold back huffing a breath. Un-freakin-believable. She didn't know why they were really stationed here, but that didn't mean Finn wasn't aware.

He wasn't her partner at all. Maybe he was the one sent to babysit her. But for the life of her, she couldn't figure out why.

"Do you think there are more?" she asked, still feigning worry. This was the part she was good at. Acting scared, acting stupid, wondering out loud. Ask a human a direct question and their instinct was to answer. Every time. Too bad for Finn she was almost as good as a shifter at sniffing out a lie. Years undercover had honed her instincts for people.

"Probably not. It's probably Damon keeping tabs on us."

If Finn really believed it was Damon, he would be pitching a way bigger fit and searching the woods for more. He was full up to his eyeballs with bullshit.

"Sooo," she drawled out, "this is nothing to worry about?"

"I don't know, Holman. I mean, shit! Do you expect me to know every answer in the goddamned world?" Defensiveness—a huge counterpart to lying. Get angry and take the focus off the fib. "What are you so worried the dragon will see, Holman? Your boyfriend sneaking in here to fuck you like an animal every night? Huh? You worried he'll see you drying your laundry, drinking a beer, or taking a fucking hike?"

She leveled him with an empty smile. "I didn't tell you where I'd found the camera, Finn."

"I don't know what you're talking about." But the whites in his eyes said he knew he was busted.

"I drink an occasional beer on the back porch. I keep the back door unlocked for Kirk to come spend time with me as he pleases. I hike in the back woods and dry my laundry on a line out behind my cabin. And somehow you knew where the camera was placed." He knew where all of them had been placed. She wanted to strangle him for whatever betrayal he was pulling. "Good fucking guess, *partner*. Get out."

"This is my post too—"

"Get out of my cabin!" she screamed,

shaking with rage as she jammed her finger toward the door.

Finn stood, hate in his eyes, teeth gritted like he loathed the sight of her. The feeling was mutual. "Our superiors have to watch you to make sure you don't fuck up again, Holman. They're making sure you're safe to be in the field. I'm here because you can't be trusted not to go psychotic again."

Lies.

Finn strode to the door and opened it wide, allowing the saturated afternoon light in. "If you hadn't fucked everything up, if you hadn't been a colossal failure, neither of us would be up here in this hell. The cameras are here because you're a worthless undercover cop who can't be integrated back into society without parameters. PTSD." Finn spat on the wooden floor. "Fuckin' weak."

He slammed the door behind him so hard it rattled the cabin. Alison squatted down and covered her ears with her hands as an anguished sob wrenched from her throat.

Lies, lies, lies!

Finn was blaming her because he was busted. This wasn't her fault. Not her fault. Riggs's gasping face slashed across her mind, and she shook her head hard to rattle the vision away. His eyes had been so scared, but he'd shaken his head slightly. *Don't help me. They'll kill you. Don't blow your cover. Don't do anything.*

And she was supposed to allow his murderer to kill the last good parts of her, too? No. She didn't regret going cold. Didn't regret going numb. Didn't regret choking the life from that man. She'd done it tearless because she'd seen too much by that time to feel pain anymore, emotional or otherwise. Kirk had watched Kong tortured, and he'd said he went dead inside...well, she knew that feeling intimately. Knew what it was like to snap. To have enough and not want to feel pain anymore, so she'd turned it off. Her feelings, her humanity, all of it. And now, her flashbacks were always the same. Riggs's face. Riggs's pain. She barely remembered killing his murderer, and for the life of her, she couldn't bring herself to feel guilty.

Oh, she knew what that said about her. She'd taken a life remorselessly.

She wasn't Ghost. She was Monster.

Finn was good at games. He knew which buttons to push. Mock her pain, mock what she'd been through, and suddenly she was falling apart instead of focusing on what she'd just learned. If he didn't place the cameras, he knew who did. Well, fuck him and whatever sketchy mission he was on.

Alison stood and strode for her room. Where there was fire, there was gasoline. Cameras wouldn't be the only thing she had to worry about. She wiped the sleeve of her hoodie over her cheeks and rifled through her drawers, turned over the bedside table, searched the lamp, the mattress, the bedframe, her suitcase. After turning her room upside down, and then the rest of the house, she found three bugs, which meant someone had been listening to every word she said to Finn. Every word she said to Kirk when he'd spent the night in here with her. They'd listened to Kirk's first *I love you*. They'd stolen private moments from her, and for what? There was no reason for her and Finn to even be here! The shifters posed no threat to anyone. They never had.

She slammed her hiking boot down on the bugs and crushed them to dust, and then she pulled her knife and cut the lining of her suitcase. She hadn't come into this weaponless. She'd come to this job just as she had any other because she would never taper her instincts again. She wouldn't feel safe as long as she was working this job.

With trembling fingers, she pulled the burner phone from the lining and turned it on, then dialed the number of someone she knew she could trust.

"Porter," her handler answered.

"It's hot as hell in here," she murmured darkly. He would get it. He always had. Porter needed to get his hands on a burner phone quick and call her back because if she was being spied on, so was her handler.

"Give me five," he muttered, and the line went dead.

She paced the tossed bedroom, chewing on her thumbnail as her mind raced. Was this about her, or about the shifters? Was it about a case she had worked? She'd built up a mass of enemies, but as far as she knew, she hadn't been outed. Her tats were a giveaway, but she hadn't gotten them until the Chicago job. Fuck, what was Finn into?

Her burner rang, and she rushed to answer. "I'm here."

"What's gone wrong?" Porter asked.

"Something's not right. I've felt it since they assigned me the job. I'm sitting here, doing nothing, waiting for something I don't understand. And then I found five cameras in the woods, all pointed at my cabin, and none around Finn's house. I thought, okay, maybe it's just security for the post, but I just asked my partner about them, and he gave me a whole lot of bullshit reasons I'm being watched. And I just disabled three bugs that were in my house."

"Shit. Did you get them all?"

"Yes. I searched every inch of this place. Can you look up Finn Brackeen's file?"

"Hang on." The sound of typing clicked over the line. Porter sighed an irritated sound. "He's clean."

"Clean? No, he had sexual harassment reports. Three of them from female officers in his precinct."

"No, Holman. If he did, that information has been wiped. In the system, he's clean as a whistle. Hang on." More typing. "Holman, you won't believe this."

"What?"

"You're in the system. Still active duty undercover."

"No, no, no, I'm not in any system. That's the fucking benefit of being undercover."

"You are, and it has no mention of your discharge, your break, the self-defense case, none of it."

Alison backed up slowly until her shoulder blades rested against the bedroom wall. Someone had gone to a lot of trouble to make her look clean. "What does this mean?"

Her handler was quiet.

"Porter, we've been working together for a lot of years. Tell me straight. What does this mean?"

"I don't know," he admitted low. "I really don't. I have to get off this phone. I'll look into it more. How do I get ahold of you?"

Her mind raced around like a hurricane. "Let me think."

"No time," Porter said in a rush. "I'll figure it out. Be careful." The line went dead, and she yanked the burner from her ear, stared at it in horror.

With a trembling breath, she dialed Kirk's number. No answer, which made perfect damn sense because he and the Boarlanders were up at the Gray Backs' landing today, rushing to make their final numbers for the last day of logging season. They would be working until dark, maybe beyond.

Her instincts were kicked up like dust in the path of a tornado. All the fine hairs had risen all over her body, her stomach was in knots, and there was this little voice at the

269

back of her mind that was saying, *Time's up. Run!*

Alison yanked her suitcase out of her closet and tossed it onto the bed. Fingers shaking, she called Kirk again from the burner phone. No answer. Shit, she didn't feel right going to Boarland Mobile Park for sanctuary without the shifters' permission. If she had Damon's number, she would call him.

Should she even go into his mountains knowing what she knew now? They had enough on their plate without an undercover cop on the run. No, Kirk would want her to stick around. She was a Boarlander, and even if that meant nothing in the eyes of human law, it meant everything to her, to Kirk, and to the crew.

A messy armload at a time, Alison shoved her clothes from the drawer into her suitcase. A couple pair of panties fell onto the floor, but fuck 'em. *Run, run, little ghost.*

She called one last time, and certain Kirk wouldn't pick up, she put it on speaker phone and set it on her bed so she could shove a knee on her overflowing suitcase and zip it up.

"Hello?"

"Kirk!"

"Ally? What's wrong? Why are you calling

from this number?"

"Are you up on the landing?"

"Yeah. Yeah, I just took a five minute break to get some water and see if you texted me. Ally, you sound panicked. Tell me what's going on."

"Something's wrong." She searched for words. What could she really tell him? He already knew something was off from the cameras he'd found, but explaining her flighty instincts were tricky. She lowered her voice and explained, "Finn knew about those cameras, and when I confronted him, he—"

The bedroom door swung open so hard it banged against the wall. Alison startled hard.

Finn looked around the room with hollow-looking eyes, blinked slowly, and dragged his fiery gaze to her. His veins were sticking out on his neck and forehead, and his face was red. He was dressed in all black, and his bullet proof vest covered his chest.

"Finn, why are you dressed in your gear?" she asked loud enough for Kirk to hear her over the phone.

Finn's hand brushed the gun at his hip, and he gave her an empty smile that failed to reach his eyes. Slowly, he pulled her holster off the peg by the door and tossed it into the room behind him. "So you don't get trigger happy on me, Holman."

Frantic, Alison scanned the immediate area for a weapon, but came up empty. Finn approached her slowly, step-by-step. He was big, and the all-black attire and fitted vest made his shoulders look wider, his waist narrower. She'd never given much thought to Finn's strength before because she'd never felt the need to size him up as an opponent. But as he pulled a capped syringe from his pocket, those days were long behind her. Finn, her own damned partner, was the biggest threat she'd ever faced.

Alison ripped the lamp off the nightstand, the cord flying forward as it pulled from the outlet, and chucked it at his head. Finn ducked, but not fast enough, and took the brunt of the shattering glass on his elbow. Alison bolted, dropped down and slid across the wood floor between his splayed legs. Glass cut her hands, but she didn't care about that. Cuts would heal, but everything in her body screamed that whatever Finn had in that syringe would be the death of her.

Help from Kirk was out. He was too far away, so it was on her to keep breathing. To keep moving. To keep fighting whatever treacherous plan Finn had hatched.

Eyes trained on her discarded holster, she lurched forward and pushed off the floor. Finn's grasp wrenched her backward by the hair, and she screamed at the unexpected pain. The arc of the syringe flashed out of the corner of her vision, and on reflex, she jammed her hand upward and hit his wrist. Alison used the second she'd bought herself to twist in his grasp. Eyes watering from the pain at the back of her head, she jammed her knee upward and racked him, and as Finn hunched over with a grunt, she slammed her forehead against his nose. A sickening crack sounded, but she wasn't done. Alison went down with him, straddled his stomach, and pummeled that broken nose with her fists. Finn curled into himself, blocking her with his forearms, and the syringe rolled across the uneven floorboards, coming to a stop in the shallow crevice between two planks.

Finn stopped defending his face long enough to grab the side of her neck and slam her against the floor beside him. In an army crawl, he scrambled toward the syringe, but Alison was faster, and gripped the body of it. It was empty, or at least it looked like it. What the hell? She scrambled away from Finn's desperate grabbing and shoved the plunger down. A tiny capsule slid from the thick needle.

"Fucking bitch!" Finn screamed. "Now you've made it worse for yourself. That was your shot to go quickly!"

Go quickly? Alison's head was ringing as she shoved off Finn. He meant die quickly. Horrified, she bolted for the capsule and stomped her shoe on top of it. A crunch sounded, and she stood back. In horror, she gasped. The wood under the green splattered liquid was disintegrating. In a rush, she scrambled to unlace her hiking boot, but her foot was on fire. She screamed as her nerves sparked with agony. She threw the shoe and it landed against the wall, the sole dissolving completely.

And now she knew who Finn was. No, not who, but what.

She turned slowly to where Finn was lurching upward, hand over his gushing nose.

"That's an IESA kill switch. You aren't a cop. You're IESA."

Finn stood up straighter and lifted his chin, looked down at her like she was nothing. "Clever girl." He stalked her, backed her into the corner.

Alison's head felt like it had been crushed, her muscles shook from the adrenaline dump and fight, and her foot hurt so bad she couldn't even bring herself to look at it as she limped backward. But all the pain cleared in the moment Finn pulled his Glock from his hip.

"Tell me why," she rasped out, her shoulder blades hitting the wall. "You owe me that much. Why are you doing this?"

"Because we can't touch the fucking dragon with no proof he takes human life!"

"I don't understand."

Finn lowered his hand from his gory face and smiled. "You aren't here to keep peace, Holman. You're here to incite a war on these mountains. Everyone in the country will back us when they hear what Damon did to you."

"Damon hasn't done anything to me!"

The low rumble of a plane motor rattled the cabin, and the roar of a tidal wave sounded against the roof. Outside, it was near dark, but she could make out the rush of water hitting the yard, dropped from above. A pungent, chemical smell burned her nose. That wasn't water. It was some sort of lighter fluid, and everything became clear in an instant.

She was going to burn, and Damon would be blamed for her death. This is why they'd cleaned the bad marks off her file. She was the perfect target. An upstanding human citizen who had devoted her life to cleaning up the streets, burned alive by an evil dragon shifter. Her picture would be splashed across the news, deeming her the face of the war.

She retched and shook her head hard to clear it because now there was the scent of something much more familiar in the air. Finn must've turned up the gas on the kitchen stove.

She'd been so desperate to get off that desk job. Of course she would be the perfect candidate. She'd marched into this job with too little information and been fine with it. And who would miss her? Her mother was serving another ten years. Her father didn't know she existed, and the only friends she had in the world were the shifters who would be destroyed by IESA.

Finn pulled a red plastic lighter from his back pocket and waved it between his forefinger and thumb, taunting her with her death. "I can't be putting bullet holes in you. Forensics, you understand. I didn't want it to be like this, but maybe I would feel worse if you hadn't fucked that shifter. They know. About the claiming mark, they know. They'll arrest Kirk. Cage him with real monsters, or maybe he'll be the first subject of the new shifter testing facility. Maybe he'll be the beginning of the new Menagerie. You should know how completely you ruined his life before you take your last breath."

"Why, Finn? Why are you a part of this?"

His lips twitched into a snarl. "Because my brother was part of the task force that came up here after the Ashe Crew. My brother!"

"Your brother is IESA?"

"Was," he said, emphasizing the word by jamming the gun closer to her. "*Was* IESA. Now he's in the belly of the dragon. Now he's nothing but ash."

"Because he was trying to annihilate an entire species, Finn. You can see that, right? They were defending themselves!"

"It's you who doesn't see, Holman. They're just animals." He shook his head, his eyes pooling with insanity as he backed out of the room. "We're gods."

She charged him, because what else could she do? He had a gun on her, sure, but it was that or death by fire and she couldn't just stand here and watch him light her up.

Time slowed as she watched Finn lift his weapon higher, training it on her forehead.

"Stop," he screamed. Oh, he didn't want to shoot her. This had to look real. It had to look like an attack from above. There was no room for bullets in IESA's plan.

She tackled him and shoved him backward until they smashed against the wall. And she fought him like an injured animal. Clawing, hitting, kicking, fighting for her life, because that damned lighter in Finn's grasp meant she would never see Kirk again. It meant she would never see her friends or Damon's mountains again. It meant the elusive happiness she'd finally found here would be nothing more but a wisp of fresh breath at the end of a dark life. And more importantly than all of that, Kirk wouldn't know the hell that was hunting him. IESA was rebuilding and was targeting Damon's mountains again.

Her life would mean nothing, and her death would hurt the people she cared about the most. She wouldn't be used like that. Not by Finn or anyone else.

Finn wrapped one hand around her throat, closing off her windpipe. He slammed her backward, and stars danced at the edges of Alison's vision as she struggled and gasped for air.

The sound of shattering glass was

deafening, and the moment slowed, frame by frame. Finn's veins protruding from his red neck, his blue eyes bloodshot and psychotic, his teeth gritted as he strangled her, the red lighter held up in his other hand, tinkling glass blasting through the air, shining like razor-edged diamonds.

And then Finn was gone. He wasn't there choking her anymore. He was flying sideways against the wall. The splintering of wood sounded as she dragged sweet oxygen into her burning lungs. A massive silverback was on Finn now, wailing on him, but Kirk didn't know the danger. Couldn't see it. Finn was trying desperately to light the fire. She scrambled toward them, but that damned flame flickered to life.

"Kirk!"

The silverback froze, powerful arm lifted mid-deathblow as the flame expanded on the gas tainted air.

Finn chuckled out a bone-chilling sound. "Worth it!" he yelled as Kirk rounded on Alison.

In an instant, the flame rolled outward with horrifying speed, and Alison grunted as Kirk's body collided with hers. With one arm, he scooped her up so fast, her stomach dipped, and a few more jerky, powerful steps and he was diving for the shattered window he'd come through. When he landed on the grass, his giant clenched hand made a sickening splat in the soaked yard. Out here, the smell of lighter fluid was overwhelming, and she gripped harder around his neck as he bolted for the woods on three arms. An earth-shattering explosion blasted heat against her face, and she watched in horror as the cabin shot rolling flames toward them. It was coming too fast, would engulf them. She screamed as the fire licked at Kirk's back, but he bunched his muscles and launched them upward. Something massive encircled her and Kirk, and they were sucked upward so hard, her breath was pushed straight out of her lungs with the force.

A deafening, prehistoric roar sounded as a massive blue dragon flapped his wings and clutched her and Kirk tighter in his claw as he aimed for the clouds. Below them, the explosion expanded and the heat from it stung her skin, but the flames didn't touch them.

Struggling to pull in air, she looked up at the belly of the dragon that had saved her and Kirk. Damon.

She was being crushed against Kirk, and

just as she thought she would pass out from their speed, Damon crested the low-lying clouds, arched his back against the forward motion and coasted on the wind. The relief at the lessened pressure was so intense, Alison rested her head against Kirk's chest. She dragged in a deep, desperate breath and let off a sob on the exhale.

Too close. That was too damned close—not only for her, but for Kirk, too. If anything had happened to him...

Alison clutched the thick black fur of his arms as her chest heaved for breath and her eyes burned with emotion. She couldn't imagine a world where he didn't exist.

"You came," she murmured, over and over again. She punched the words through her crying as she tried to convince herself she was still alive. That she was still here with him.

Kirk's blazing eyes pooled with worry as he searched her face and ran his knuckle along the stinging cuts the glass had made.

"I'll be okay," she promised thickly.

And it was true. The words weren't just a balm to her mate's worry.

Because of Kirk and Damon, she was going to be okay.

# TWENTY-ONE

In the last streaks of sunset light, Damon lowered them carefully to the clearing at Boarland Mobile Park. The wind from his wings kicked up tornadoes of dirt, but the chaos at the trailer park didn't stop to watch. Harrison and the others were loading the bed of his truck with shovels and barrels of water, yelling and pointing, ordering each other about with panic on their faces. Even Clinton blasted by on a bobcat, complete focus in his eyes.

When Damon released them too high up, she yelped, but Kirk had her, and he landed them on the gravel with grace and an easy impact. Kirk's Change back to his human form happened before Damon had flown away, and he instantly folded her in his arms and bolted for his trailer.

"Tell me you're okay," he rushed out, eyes wild as he set her on the bed inside. "Tell me now, Ally, or I can't leave."

"Where are you going?"

"Those assholes set an uncontrolled fire with fire accelerant." He shoved his legs into a pair of jeans and whipped his hair from his face as he pulled on a shirt. "There's a reason we don't have logging season in the summer. Too hot, too dry, and any heat from our machinery could spark a forest fire. If we don't keep this contained, Damon's mountains, our homes, everything goes up in flames. Tell me you're okay, Ally."

"I'm okay, I swear."

He checked her bruised neck, lifted her shirt and examined her aching ribs, then lingered at the bottom of her foot. She still didn't want to look. Especially not after he gritted out a sigh and muttered, "Fuckin' IESA." Kirk kissed her hard and quick, and when he pulled away, he said, "I'm hitching a ride with Harrison and the boys. If we don't contain the fire and it heads for the river, you and the girls go deeper into the mountains. Up to the Gray Backs, then to the Ashe Crew territory. Gather the women and kids we're leaving behind and make sure they all get up to Damon's house safe. If it reaches you there, you take everyone into the cave under the falls beside Damon's house. We'll find you. Do you understand? Harrison will have called the smoke jumpers and the rangers outside of Damon's land. I don't want to leave you. Not now."

"Go Kirk. Help them save the park. You have to help them save the mountains."

Kirk leaned forward and kissed her hard, let his lips linger a moment, then pulled back and strode for the doorway.

"Kirk!"

He turned. "Yeah, Ally Cat?"

"Thank you for coming for me."

He smiled a sad smile as he flicked his gaze to her foot, then back to her face. "Always. I love you."

And damn it all if that didn't sound like a goodbye. He'd been careful with those words, and as he bolted from the trailer, she doubled over the pain in her chest. That was his second *I love you*, and she hoped with everything she had that it wasn't his last.

She hobbled her aching body to the front of his trailer and onto the porch just as the trucks were speeding out of the park. Kirk was in the front seat of Harrison's jacked-up red pickup with a map in his hands, talking, but when they passed, he looked up and watched her as she lifted her fingers in a wave.

Mason was in the back of the truck and called out, "I'll get him back home to you." His eyes were blazing the bright blue of his boar people as the truck sped away and disappeared into the Boarland woods.

Audrey stood quietly by Emerson, just below Kirk's porch, watching them leave.

"They're trained for fire," Emerson said, cradling her stomach with one hand and holding a small camera in the other. She lifted her attention to Alison. She looked so scared. "Fire is always a risk up here, but they know what to do. They'll be back."

In the distance, against the darkening sky, was a plume of black smoke, wide and ominous. She could smell it from here. Too close for comfort, and she knew what the heat of those flames had felt like licking at her skin. The shifters of Damon's mountains were charging the fire to save what they'd built here.

And for what? Because IESA didn't like them? Because they were scared that they weren't the top predator on earth? IESA was smoke. Dark, dangerous, able to fit in any space. Choking, poisonous, blinding.

"What are you taping?" Alison asked.

Emerson let off a trembling breath and tried to smile, but failed. "Everything. Cora said to catch what I can. I don't know much about videotaping, though. I've just been trying to document life around here for my baby to watch later. And now Bash and the boys are headed down there to that fire, and I'm here doing nothing. Ally, they're everything and we're stuck here doing nothing!"

Audrey was shaking her head, her eyes rimmed with tears, swallowing over and over like she was trying not to retch.

Hissing at the pain in her foot, Alison scrambled down the stairs, leaning heavily on the railing. "Do you want to do something big instead?"

Emerson turned, the wind whipping her black curls. She dragged her wide-eyed attention down Alison's body like she hadn't seen her before now. Her clothes were singed, and her face probably had a dozen cuts from the glass. "Ally, you look awful."

Alison snorted. "Thank you. So...what do you say?"

"To what?"

"Do you want to do something big? Something that will make a difference for our people." *Our people.* Alison would do anything for them.

"What did you have in mind?" Audrey asked.

"An interview. You can ask me questions about tonight." Alison jerked her chin toward the smoke. "IESA thinks I'm dead. I can blow their operation wide open with what I know."

"But Ally," Emerson said, her cheeks pale in the dim evening light. "If they think you're dead, you could escape. Go underground, change your appearance. *Live.* You can't go on television. You're the Ghost."

Alison stared at the billowing black that was polluting the sky. Something irreplaceable was being taken from these people, and the world should see what was really happening. They should know why the shifters were having their rights stripped, why she'd been sent here. She had never been a peacekeeper as she'd thought. She'd been a war machine.

The country had revolted about IESA when Cora Keller had exposed them the first time, proof that there was more good than bad in this world. They would rally again if they had the facts. If they knew IESA was rebuilding.

Here was where Alison was going to make her stand. These people deserved to stop taking blows at the whim of a scared government.

She would stop running for Kirk. For the people here. For herself.

With fire in her soul, Alison locked eyes on Emerson and murmured, "I'm not a ghost anymore."

# TWENTY-TWO

Today had been the most hellish day of his life, and that was saying something. Kirk tossed an exhausted glance to the back seat where Bash was stretched out and dozing in and out with his face against the window. He was covered in soot, just like Mason and Clinton, who sat in the bed of Harrison's truck, staring off into the woods with haunted looks in their eyes.

"You want to talk about it?" Harrison asked in a hoarse voice. Yelling orders and breathing thick smoke all night did that.

"Talk about what?"

"About what happened to Ally."

Kirk winced against the vision of her being choked by that asshole partner of hers. He'd barely resisted the urge to rip that fucker limb from limb. "Won't help."

Bash stirred and gripped Kirk's shoulder too rough. "Talking always helps. Harrison and me both learned that."

Kirk sighed an irritated sound and said, "Fine. She called me when I was up on the landing. You saw that."

"Saw you blur out of there in Clinton's new truck," Harrison muttered. "I thought he was going to bleed us all he was so pissed. And you screamed for us to call Damon, but I didn't know what to tell him. I just knew Ally was in trouble."

"I could hear her," Kirk whispered, shaking his head just to get a grip on the pain in his middle the memory caused. "I had my phone sitting on the seat, and I could hear her fighting for her life, trying to give me hints about what was happening, and I thought I wasn't going to get to her in time." He ripped his attention away from the road illuminated in soft, early dawn light. "I thought I was going to lose her. And she fought, Harrison. She was still fighting when I got to her."

"You got yourself a badass mate," Bash murmured. "That Ally girl, she's a fighter."

Kirk swallowed hard and nodded. "Brackeen had turned the gas on in the house, and someone had dumped fire accelerant in a straight line over the cabins, like they were trying to make it look like a scorch mark from dragon's fire. It was all a setup, and Ally was the one supposed to take the fall." Kirk clenched his hands and closed his eyes tightly against the urge to Change and rip up the forest just to quell the red rage inside of him. "Finn had an IESA kill switch for her, and when she fought that off, they were gonna burn her alive, Harrison. Imagine how you would feel if someone tried to do that to Audrey." He gave Bash a glance over his shoulder. "Imagine if they tried to do it to Emerson and your baby. You are my crew. Ally is my family group. I want to kill all those mother fuckers."

Harrison's cell phone rang. He answered it and put it on speaker phone as he pulled under the Boarland Mobile Park sign. "Cora, you're on speaker."

"Hey boys."

"Hey Cora," they all said in unison, even Clinton and Mason in the back. Shifter hearing didn't suck.

"Are you guys around a television?"

"About to be," Harrison said. "Why?"

"Because Kirk's mate has a massive set of lady balls, and she's about to shake up the damned world."

Kirk frowned and leaned forward. "What do you mean?"

"You'll see. Just get in front of a television and turn on the news."

"Local?"

"No, Harrison. National. Ally sent me something to put on the air. Something big." There was a smile in her voice when she said, "You call me after and tell me how you like my editing. And Kirk?"

"Yeah, Cora?"

"You done good, boy." Her voice was teasing, light, and didn't make any damned sense, but before he could ask, the line went dead.

Harrison gave him a what the hell look and pulled straight through the trailer park to 1010 where the front door was standing wide open.

Every instinct in Kirk's body told him to get to his mate. To touch her and hold her and convince his gorilla she was all right, but he smelled like smoke, and his boots were muddy from where the ash had mixed with the water and turned to thick, pungent glop.

On the porch of 1010, he peeled off his ruined shirt and kicked out of his boots, then stumbled through the front door into the soft glow of the living room lamp.

Emerson, Audrey, and Ally were sitting shoulder to shoulder on the couch. They twisted around with expectant looks on their faces. Audrey and Emerson got up and bolted for their mates, but Ally looked exhausted and winced when she tried. Had to be her foot hurting. It had a bad chemical burn all across her sole. He hoped she didn't carry the limp forever, but she might.

Ally's eyes had dimmed to a stormy blue and were hollow, and though someone had cleaned the cuts on her face, her skin was pale as a phantom. Kirk was haunted by the vision of her being hurt, sure, but she'd actually lived through Finn's attack and betrayal. His chest rattled with a helpless noise as he strode around the couch and sank down beside her.

"Shhhh," she whispered, pulling him closer and pressing her hand against his rattling chest. She rocked him gently like he was the one who needed comfort right now. Nurturing mate, caring for everyone else above herself. God, he loved her more than anything in the world.

On the glowing television was footage of the fire. A grainy, faraway picture of Damon's massive dragon flying away from the explosion flashed across the screen, and a subtitle ran constantly across the bottom of the frame. *Damon Daye murdered a human police officer.* A picture of Ally appeared in the top right corner as a reporter listed her accomplishments in the field. In the picture, Ally had long brunette hair, her chin lifted proudly, and she looked striking in her police uniform.

"That feels like it was taken a million years ago," she murmured.

Kirk sighed and dragged her against his side. "They think Brackeen's body is yours. They think you're dead."

She huffed a soft laugh and nodded once. "Yeah, well, they won't think that for long."

*Breaking News* flashed across the bottom of the screen, and the news reporter pressed her fingertips to her ear and said, "We have new information regarding the fire in Damon's mountains."

"Here it is," Emerson said nervously. "Turn it up."

Kirk leaned forward, plucked the remote off the coffee table, and hit the volume button.

In the video, Ally sat on the couch where they were now sitting, the lamplight soft against her cheeks as she wrung her hands nervously. Her lips twitched into a smile, then fell as Emerson asked her from off camera, "Please state your name and what you do."

"Uuuh, it's the middle of the night on June sixteenth. Outside, there is a fire raging and threatening the mountains here. My name is Alison Holman. Officer Alison Holman," she corrected with a nervous laugh. She looked straight into the camera and murmured, "And no matter what anyone is saying, I am most certainly not dead."

"You were at that fire tonight?"

"Yes."

The crinkle of paper turning sounded. "Was it Damon Daye who set that fire?"

"No. Damon Daye saved me from that fire."

"Who..." Emerson cleared her throat and murmured, "I'm sorry. I'm really nervous."

Ally smiled and said, "It's okay. Just pretend it's me and you."

Emerson swallowed noisily as the camera panned to her. Audrey must've been filming. Emerson stood, sat next to Ally, and gripped her hand. "You're my friend, and it's hard to see you hurt. Last night, you were attacked unprovoked by your own partner. Choked. Chemically burned by a kill switch. And then

BOARLANDER SILVERBACK | T. S. JOYCE

someone doused your cabin in fire accelerant, filled it with gas, and lit a lighter. Who did this to you?"

"IESA. Not Damon Daye." Ally's face went stern, and her voice steadied. And then his strong-as-steel woman launched into the story of what happened. She didn't embellish, didn't exaggerate. She said it straight and missed nothing. She didn't let IESA off the hook for a single thing.

"Why would they do this?" Emerson asked.

"Because my death was supposed to frame Damon Daye and cause war with the shifters. Shifters have been stripped of some of their rights already, and you have to ask yourself why. Don't listen blindly to what the media feeds you," she urged. "Do your research. Demand responsible coverage. Open your mind to the possibility that while shifters aren't exactly like humans, they still care about the same things."

The scene cut to a video of them at the falls. Of Ally sitting in Kirk's lap, smiling at him like he was the most important part of her world. Emerson turned the camera on herself and Bash, kissed his cheek, and then laughed as he cupped her belly and nuzzled her neck affectionately.

296

Ally's voice came on over the playful scene. "They care about love. Family. They care about friendships."

There was a slow motion shot of the Boarlanders jumping off the falls together, grins on their faces. There was a close-up of Ally and Kirk's hands, holding tight as they walked through the woods. The little heart tattoo on Ally's wrist that Kirk loved to kiss was pink and perfect against her skin.

"They aren't here to hurt anyone. They're trying to live, just like everyone else."

The screen faded to black and opened again with Harrison's grinning face as he gave Audrey a piggy-back ride through the woods, her pink flip-flops dangling from her fingers as she cheesed and waved at the camera.

"They want what everyone else wants," Ally said in a thickening voice. She appeared on camera again, clutching Emerson's hand. Her eyes were rimmed with tears as she murmured, "They want to be free."

The screen faded to black, and the reporter sat there, looking stunned.

"Holy hell," Harrison murmured from behind the couch where his arms were locked on the back of it as he stared in shock at the screen.

"I like your heart tattoo," Bash said in a happy voice. "Looks real good on the TV. And Emerson, you looked hot as fuck. And Audrey, you held the camera real good."

Mason gripped Ally's shoulder. "It's good to have you in our corner." He shook her gently and lowered his voice. "Damon is important to me, and you risked yourself to protect him. You need anything—anything at all—just ask." His voice cracked on the last word, and then he abruptly left 1010.

Clinton ruffled Ally's hair roughly from behind the couch and made to leave, but stopped. Slowly, he turned and grabbed her hand. He searched Ally's face and said, "You ain't no C-Team today. You're A-Team Ally." He squeezed her palm once, then walked out behind Mason, leaving Ally staring after him with shocked, wide eyes.

Kirk watched as the rest of their crew gave her hugs, and murmured their thanks. It struck him what she'd done. She hadn't sat here waiting for them to come back from fighting that fire. She and the girls had gone to work, and done more good than he could've ever imagined.

Kirk hugged her tightly as the first blinding rays of sunlight filtered through the open window of 1010. How fitting after the hell they'd been through that the sun shone through the smoke and smog that thickened the air.

It reminded him of his Ally. Of her resilience. He was so damned proud of her.

She wasn't hiding anymore. She wasn't a ghost. She wasn't invisible.

Instead, she'd gone to battle for him and for the shifters of Damon's mountains.

Kirk pulled her into his lap, desperate to be closer to her, and she slid her arms around his neck and buried her face against his chest. Her shoulders shook with emotion, and it ripped him up inside. They'd both been scared of losing each other last night.

Cupping her cheek, Kirk lifted her gaze to his so she could see the truth in his eyes when he said, "I see you, Ally."

She smiled as a single, glistening tear streamed down her cheek. "I love you, too."

# TWENTY-THREE

Over the course of a month, Alison's life had done a complete turnaround.

One month since the fire. One month since going on the attack against IESA. One month since the petitions and picket lines had flared around the country in support of shifters. One month since the government backpedaled and decided to hold a vote within the year to reinstate shifter rights.

She had resigned from the police force, but Porter had come to her aid and publically backed her. On behalf of his precinct, he'd denounced any further involvement with IESA, no matter what the superiors ordered. Sacrificing one of their own had given shifters an unexpected ally.

Alison stood up on her four-wheeler and scanned the woods, but all was quiet. God, it was so stunning out here. She was surrounded by thick, towering pines and birds singing in the canopy. Green moss and ground cover made these woods feel like a jungle, and everywhere she looked, there was an incredible mountain view. She didn't miss the noise of the city anymore. In fact, she couldn't remember very clearly her life before meeting Kirk. Her past was a blur, while her present was crisp and defined. Beautiful.

It had been one month since Damon had hired her to run security for his land.

She waved at Georgia as the park ranger slowed on the trail, headed back to the tree house ranger station Beaston had built for her.

"Headed home?" Georgia asked.

*Home.* The sound of that word never ceased to warm her from the inside out. "Yeah. Kirk says he has a surprise for me," she said excitedly.

Georgia snorted. "When Jason says that, it's usually his dick. His dick is the surprise."

Alison giggled and waved as Georgia sped off into the woods.

She hit the gas on her ATV and blasted toward home. A familiar feeling washed over her as she drove under the Boarland Mobile Park sign. It was the same sensation she always felt when she came back to this place after work. It was a feeling of such deep-rooted belonging that, like always, her heart pounded a little harder.

Clinton sat in a plastic lawn chair with a silver suntanning screen resting on his chest as he looked up at the sky in his yellow trucker hat with a red rope candy hanging from his mouth. He didn't greet her as she passed, but he also didn't flip her off, which was progress.

Bash, Emerson, Harrison, and Audrey were cooking what smelled like hamburgers on the new built-in grill the boys had constructed where the old ant pile used to be, and their laughter echoed across the park. On his porch, Mason nodded a greeting to her and plucked soft notes on his old guitar. He would leave here soon and move into Damon's house when it was finished, and a wave of sadness took her. He would be missed. Already, she felt a hole in her chest from his absence.

Usually she rode straight back to 1010 where she and Kirk had been staying, but today, he sat on the steps of his own trailer, the first one on the left. His long legs were bent, his muscular arms draped over his knees, his long hair fallen forward as he gave her one of those breathtaking crooked smiles.

She still couldn't believe he was hers.

"Did you finish the trailer?" she asked hopefully.

"Maybe," he teased.

With an excited squeal, she cut the engine and bolted for him. He caught her and spun her in a slow circle.

"That isn't your surprise, though." He settled her on her feet and pulled up the sleeve of his white T-shirt. Down the inside of his bicep, in perfect script, was a tattoo that read *ghost*.

"You got a tattoo for me?" she asked, heart in her throat as she traced the new ink. It was his first.

He pulled her hand up, then kissed the small, neat letter *K* that she'd had done just beside her pink heart. "I know we can't show everyone your claiming mark. The world isn't ready yet, but this we can do. This claiming mark is legal."

"Okay," she said thickly. She couldn't even put into words how much this meant to her.

"You ready to see our trailer?"

"Yeah." He'd been working on it non-stop lately, but hadn't allowed her to see the inside.

Kirk led her up the steps, and just before he opened the beautifully stained dark wooden door, he said, "Close your eyes."

She did and clutched onto his bicep as they stepped inside. It still smelled of sawdust and new paint.

Kirk sipped her lips and whispered, "Okay, Ally Cat. Open them."

Alison gasped as she spun in a slow circle, scanning their home. Kirk had opened up all the walls and supported the new ceiling with natural wood beams. The large bedroom area took up one third of the home on the right, there was an open living room in the center with refurbished chestnut wood floors. There was wainscoting and designer paint in different shades of gray, and even the couch and coffee table looked new, perfect in the space. She laughed at the large painted picture of a gorilla ripping the cord of a chainsaw under a rainbow. It looked like a six year old made it, and in the bottom right-hand corner, Willa had signed her name. It added the perfect amount of interest and color on the long back wall. The kitchen was the real showstopper, though. It had glistening granite countertops, antique white cabinets, and a large farmhouse sink. It looked like it belonged in some fancy magazine.

"I wish I could give you more. You deserve

more," Kirk said from behind her. "But this is what I have to give. A refurbished trailer home, a C-Team crew of shifters...and me."

"That's more than enough, Kirk. It's everything."

She turned to hug him, but he wasn't where she'd expected. Instead, he was down on one knee, a white gold band encircled with tiny, shimmering diamonds in his hand.

She clasped her hands over her mouth to keep the sob in her throat and blinked hard to keep her tears at bay.

His smile was big and his eyes sincere as he uttered the words, "We can't marry right now, but someday, things will be different for us. I *know* they will. And until then, I'd be honored if you wore my ring. Ally..."

"Yeah?" she asked in a small voice.

"Will you have me as your husband?"

With a jerky nod, she dropped down to him and hugged his neck as tight as she could. He rocked them gently and massaged slow circles on her back.

This was it.

This was the moment she would cherish for always. The moment Kirk had chosen her in every possible way. She hadn't known what family—real family—was before she'd stumbled into Boarland woods that first night, but Kirk had known just what she needed and had given it to her.

A home, a crew...him.

He didn't think he had much to offer, but he didn't see. Before him, her life had been lacking. It had been dark and hard, but he'd come in and made it blindingly beautiful.

From now until forever, she would never have to question where she belonged.

No matter what happened from here on, she would face it beside the man who had fought for this moment and earned her heart.

# Want More of the Boarlanders?

The Complete Series is Available Now

Other books in this series:

## Boarlander Boss Bear
(Boarlander Bears, Book 1)

## Boarlander Bash Bear
(Boarlander Bears, Book 2)

## Boarlander Beast Boar
(Boarlander Bears, Book 4)

## Boarlander Cursed Boar
(Boarlander Bears, Book 5)

# About the Author

T.S. Joyce is devoted to bringing hot shifter romances to readers. Hungry alpha males are her calling card, and the wilder the men, the more she'll make them pour their hearts out. She werebear swears there'll be no swooning heroines in her books. It takes tough-as-nails women to handle her shifters.

Experienced at handling an alpha male of her own, she lives in a tiny town, outside of a tiny city, and devotes her life to writing big stories. Foodie, wolf whisperer, ninja, thief of tiny bottles of awesome smelling hotel shampoo, nap connoisseur, movie fanatic, and zombie slayer, and most of this bio is true.

Bear Shifters? Check
Smoldering Alpha Hotness? Double Check
Sexy Scenes? Fasten up your girdles, ladies and gents, it's gonna to be a wild ride.

For more information on T. S. Joyce's work,
visit her website at
www.tsjoycewrites.wordpress.com

27588000R00171

Printed in Great Britain
by Amazon